BUSNESS STUDIES CLASS-XII

- **Exam Revision Notes**
- **Lecture Freely available on Youtube"**

Dhruvkant Sharma

Pharos Books

ISBN: 978-93-89843-42-2

Publisher: **Pharos Books Private Limited**
Address: A-55, Main Mother Dairy Road,
                 Pandav Nagar, East Delhi-110092
Phone: +91 8447931000, 9319228272
E-mail: sales@pharosbooks.in
Website: www.pharosbooks.in
Facebook: www.facebook.com/pharosbooks.in
Edition: 2020

Business Studies
By- Dhruvkant Sharma

INDEX

From author- Don't Expect Anything Arom Anybody. Take Control of Your Destiny. Believe in Yourself. Please Avoid Negative Sources, People, Places and Habits.

MANAGEMENT: (4 to 8 marks)

Management is the process of planning, organising, staffing, directing & controlling the resources efficiently and effectively for achieving the organisation goals.

Or

Management is a process of getting things done in an effective manner.

e.g.:-CWG games in Delhi, Indian railway management, management in your home during marriage or other occasions

EFFECTIVENESS:

Means doing a particular task in given time or achieving given target but at **higher production cost.**

In this manager uses more labor cost and other input to be effective.

e.g.- target of 10000 unit of nano

For this working doubled by day and night due to power failure target achieve but production cost went so high.

$$\text{Effectiveness} = \frac{\text{Achieved}}{\text{Desired}}$$

EFFICIENCY:

Businessman concentrates more on producing goods with **fewer resources.** In this cost goes down but target cannot achieved.

e.g. - out of 10000 unit of nano, every nano produced will cost minimum cost with fewer resources whether target achieve or not.

✄ Features of management

1. **Goal oriented process-** Organisation has a set of goal to achieve.
2. **Pervasive-** performed in all type of organisation
3. **Continuous-** series of continuous, composite but separate functions.

4. **Dynamic in nature-** organisation must change itself according to need of the environment.
5. **Intangible-** cannot be seen but its presence can be felt.
6. **Group activity-** organisation is group of individuals who work together in team spirit.
7. **Multi-dimensional -** (work, people, operations)

◆ **Management process/ function :-**

1.   Planning

2.   Organising

3.   Staffing

4.   Directing

5.   Controlling

✂ **Objectives of management**

Organisational (GPS)	Social (society)	Personal (employee)
Survival– Must earn enough revenues to cover costs.	Environment friendly product social objectives involve the creation of bene-fits for the society.	Competitive salary Personal objectives are related to the employees of the organisations.
Profit – Profit is essential for covering costs and risks of the business.	employment	Peer recognition
Growth- Every business needs to add to its prospects in the long run.	Basic amenities	Personal growth

◆ **Importance of management (why management is necessary)**

1.   Help in achieving group goal

2.   Increase efficiency

3. Help In achieving personal objective
4. Help In development of society
5. Create a dynamic organisation

✂ Nature of management as an art, as a science and as a profession

As a science	As an Art	As a profession
Science is a systematic body of knowledge that explain certain general truth or the operation of general laws.	Art is the skillful and personal application of existing knowledge to achieve desired result.	Profession is well defined body of knowledge approved by professional association.
Systematic body of knowledge	Existence of theoretical knowledge	Well defined body of knowledge
Principal based experiments	Personalised application	Restricted entry
Universal validity	Based on continuous practice	Professional association
	creativity	Ethical code of conduct
		Service motive
Conclusion- management is an inexact science	**Conclusion-** Yes, but cannot be said to be pure art.	**Conclusion-** not full fledges profession.

✂ Levels of management with functions:-

Levels	Top level management	Middle level management	Third/operational level management / lower level / supervisory level

example	CEO, CFO, CHAIRMAN, PRESIDENT. VP,GM	HRM, PM, DM, OM, FM.	FOREMAN, SUPERVISOR CLEARK
functions	1. Formulate plan	1. Interpret the policy	1. Oversee the efforts of workforce
	2. Coordinate activity	2. Assign duty	2. Interact with actual workforce
	3. Responsible for welfare	3. Motivate employees	3. Maintain quality of output

COORDINATION:

It is the process of achieving unity of action among interdependence activities and departments of an organisation.

E.g.: Finance department, HR department and Marketing all require coordination.

◆ **This fact is highlighted through the following discussion:-**

1. Coordination in planning
2. Coordination in organising
3. Coordination in staffing
4. Coordination in directing
5. Coordination in controlling

◆ **Nature /Characteristics /Features of coordination**

1. Integrate group efforts
2. Ensure unity of action
3. Continuous process
4. All pervasive function
5. Deliberate function
6. Responsibility of all managers

◆ **Need and importance of coordination [kyo Karen coordinate]**

1. Growth in size
2. Specialisation
3. Functional differentiation
4. Interdependence of different processes

From Author- "Don't Work For Money, Happiness is The Basic Purpose of Life.

PRINICIPLES OF MANAGEMENT: (6-8 marks)

Principals of management are broad general guidelines for managerial decision-making and behavior.

Management principals are derived on the basis of observation and analysis of events and by conducting experimental studies.

Eg: - law of gravity, law of Pythagoras and law of five finger etc.

Features of management-

1.	**general guidelines**
2.	**formed by experiments and practice**
3.	**contingent** – The application of management principles is contingent or dependent upon the prevailing situation at a particular point of time. The application of principles has to be changed as per requirements.
4.	**Flexible** – They can be modified by the manager to meet the demand of the situation.
5.	universal applicability
6.	cause and effect relationship
7.	behavioral

✂ **Significance /importance of management-**

1.	provide useful insight reality
2.	optimum utilisation of resources (3M)
3.	scientific decision
4.	meeting changing environment requirement
5.	fulliing social responsibility
6.	management training (on the job, off the job)

✂ **Fayol principal of management (for explanation refer book)**

1.	division of work and specialisation
2.	authority and responsibility (ch.organising)
3.	discipline
4.	unity of command (one boss one head)
5.	unity of direction (one boss one plan)
6.	subordination of individual interest to general interest
7.	remuneration of employee (just and equitable)

8.	centralisation and decentralisation (ch.organising)
9.	scalar chain (ch.directing ...communication)
10.	stability of personnel (don't move)
11.	order
12.	equity (no discrimination)
13.	initiative (first step by own)
14.	esprit de corps (unity is strength)

✂ Different Between Unity Of Command And Unity Of Direction

Basis of Difference	Unity of Command	Unity of Direction
1. Aim	It prevents dual subordination.	It prevents overlapping of various activities.
2. Implications	It affects an individual employee.	It affects the entire organisation.

SCIENCETIFIC MANAGEMENT:

"Scientific management means knowing exactly what you want men to do and seeing that they do it in the best and cheapest way"

-F.W. Taylor

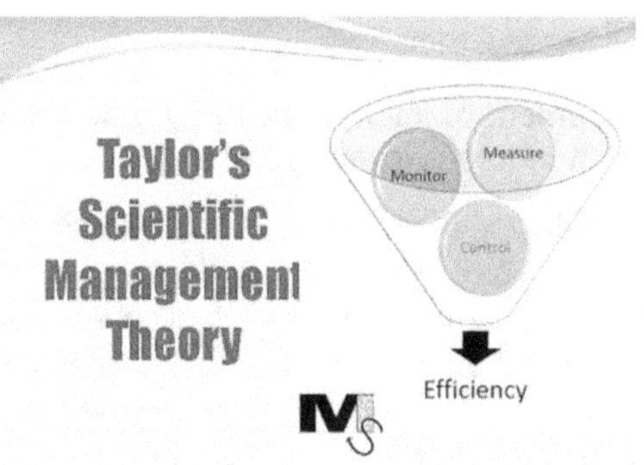

It means conducting business activities according to standardised tools, methods & trained personal in order to increase the output, improve quality & reduce the cost & wastes.

◆ Taylor scientific principal of management-

1. Science not rule of thumb:

Taylor believed that there was only one best method to maximise efficiency. The method can be developed through study and analysis. The method developed should substitute 'Role of Thumb' (or trial) and error approach) throughout the organisation.

2. Harmony not discard:

Taylor emphasised that there should be complete harmony between the management and the workers. To achieve this, Taylor advocated a complete 'Mental Revolution i.e., a change in the attitude of workers and management towards one another from competition to cooperation. Both should realise that they require one another.

3. Cooperation not individualism:

According to this principle, there should be complete cooperation between labour and management instead of individualism or competition. This principle is an extension of principle of 'harmony, not discord'. Manager should reward the employees for their suggestions which results in substantial reduction in costs.

4. Development of each and every person to his/her greatest efficiency and prosperity

According to Taylor, to increase efficiency each person should be scientifically selected and the work assigned should suit his/her physical, mental and intellectual capabilities. They should be given the required training to learn the' best method' to do a job.

5. Maximum, not restricted output:

Continuous increase in production and productivity is another basic principle of scientific management. The aim of both workers and management should be to maximize output.

⌘ Scientific technique of taylor-

1.	Functional foremanship (like division of work)
2.	Standardisation and simplification of work
3.	Method study (one best method)
4.	Motion study (ineffective motions)
5.	Time study **(stop watch)**
6.	Fatigue study **(give rest)**
7.	Differential piece wage system **(bonus and incentives)**
8.	Mental Revolution

☞ Functional foremanship

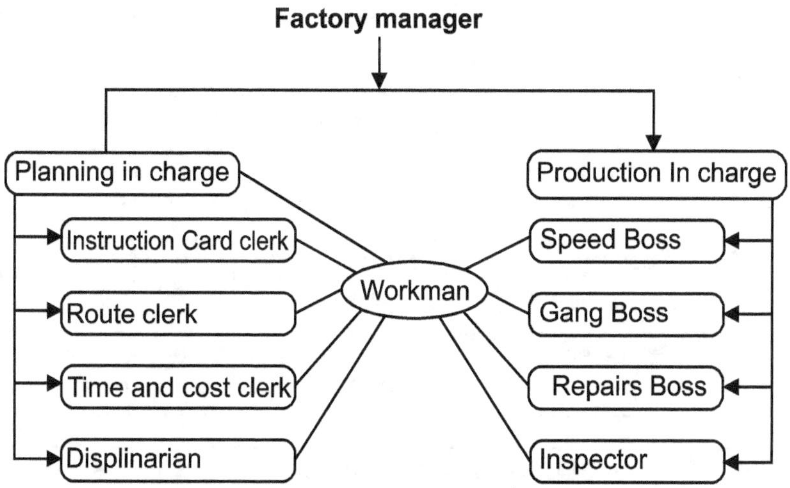

◆ Role of foremen under planning in charge

- ☞ Instruction card clerk ---Drafting instruction for workers
- ☞ Route clerk --- Specifying the route of production.
- ☞ Time and cost clerk --- Preparing time and cost sheet.
- ☞ Disciplinarian ---- Ensuring discipline

◆ Role of foremen under production in charge

- ☞ Speed boss ---- Timely and accurate completion of job
- ☞ Gang boss ---- Keeping machines and tools ect. Ready for operation by workers
- ☞ Repairs boss ---- Ensuring proper working condition of machines and tools
- ☞ Inspectors ---- Checking the quality of work

✵ DIFFERENCE BETWEEN HENRY FAYOL AND F.W.TAYLOR

	BASIS	HENRI FAYOL	FW.TAYLOR
1	personality	practitioner	Scientist
2	Basis of formation	Personal experience	Observation and experimentation
3	Perspective	Top level management	Shop floor level of factory
4	Applicability	Universal	Specialised situations
5	Focus	Improving overall administration	Increasing productivity
6	Expression	General theory of administration	Scientific management

From Author- "Daily Chant Yourself That I am The Best and I Can do it, I am in Top of The World"

BUSINESS ENVIRONMENT: (3-5 marks)

Business environment means the sum total of all individuals, institutions and other forces that are outside the control of a business enterprise but they may affect its performance.

Eg: - Alaknanda market, Saket mall and Karol bagh has different environment for business.

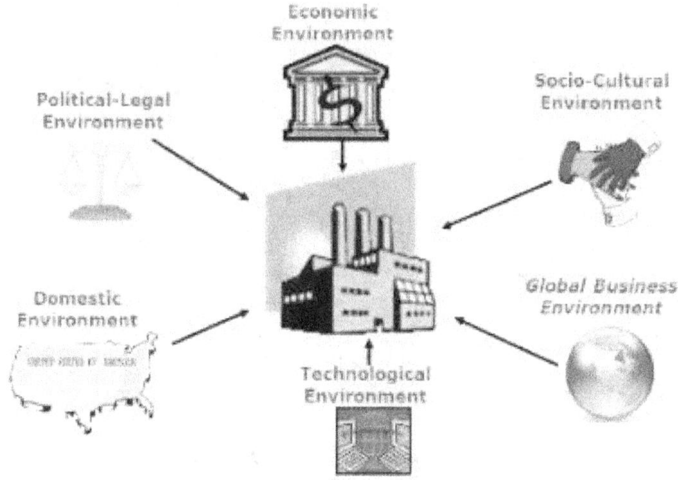

◆ The complete awareness and understanding of business environment is known as **environment scanning.**

◆ **Features of business environment**

1. Complexity

2. Dynamic

3. Specific and general forces

4. Uncertainty

5. Relativity

◆ **Importance of business environment (SWOT)**

1. Help to find opportunities

2. Help to identify threats

3. Help in planning and policy formation
4. Help in tapping useful resources
5. Help in coping with rapid changes
6. Help in improving performance

⌘ **Dimension /components /elements of business environment (for explanation refer book)**

Business Environment
Economic Environment
Social Environment
Technological Environment
Political Environment
Legal Environment

1. **Economics environment:-** Inflation rate, interest rates, value of rupee, stock market indices.

2. **Social environment**:- Custom and tradition society expectations from business values.

3. **Political environment**:- Stability peace attitude of elected government

4. **Legal environment:-** Laws made by government Courts judgments

   Eg. Advertisement on packets of cigarettes.

5. **Technological environment (BSNL, JIO)**:- Innovation in the

market new method of operation

Eg. Cassettes, CD, pen drive, mobile.

◆ **Government Policy in 1991**

LIBERALISATION: (Making doing business easy)

Liberalisation means freeing the Indian business and industry (especially for private sectors) from all unnecessary govt. control and restrictions.

E.g.-freedom in fixing the prices, Reduction is tax rate, abolishing licensing etc.

PRIVATISATION:

Privatisation means giving greater role to the private sector in the nation building process and drastically reducing the role of the public sector.

To achieve this the govt. adopted the policy of planned disinvestment which means transferring the public sector enterprises to the private sector.

Eg. Recently government of announce 100% FDI in some sector in Indian business.

GLOBALISATION: (whole word one market)

Globalisation means integration of labour, capital, technology and other resources of one economy to world's another economy. In short globalisation means the integration of our economy with the word economy.

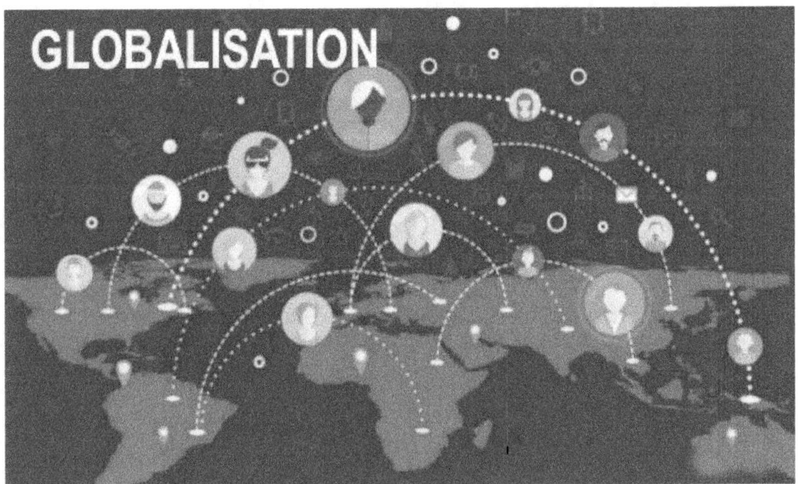

◆ **Major steps of economic reforms:-**

1.   New industrial policy

2.   New trade policy

3.   Fiscal reforms

4.   Monetary reforms

5.   Capital market reforms

6.   Dismantling price control

DEMONETISATION (FRESH TOPIC ADDED)

The govt. of India announced 'Demonetisation' of the two largest denomination currency notes, Rs. 500 and rs. 1000. As a result, the existing rs.500 and rs.1000 currency notes ceased to be legal tender. This led to 86% of the money in circulation invalid.

Demonetisation is the act of the government to cancel the legal tender status of a currency unit in circulation.

The aim of demonetisation was to curd corruption, counterfeiting the use of the high denomination notes for illegal activities; and especially the accumulation of 'black money' generated by income that has not been declared to the tax authorities.

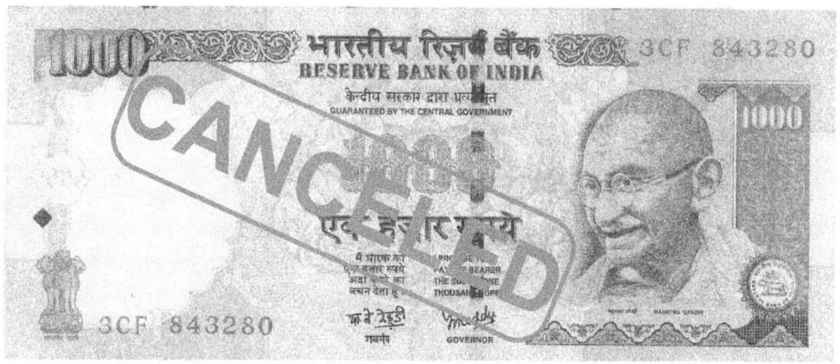

◆ Features of Demonetisation

1.   Demonetisation is viewed as a tax administration measure.

Cash holdings arising from declared income was readily deposited in the banks and exchange for new notes . but those with black money had to declare their unaccounted wealth and pay taxes at a penalty rate.

2. **Demonetisation is also interpreted as a measure to improve tax compliance.**

   It indicated that tax evasion will no longer be tolerated or accepted. Tax collection increased because of increased disclosure. Tax evasion decreased.

3. **demonetisation also led to channelising savings into the formal financial system.**

   Bank deposits increased. However , interest rates decreased.

4. **Demonetization is aimed to create a less-cash or cash lite economy.**

   Cash transactions declined. Digital transactions increased involving the use of RuPay cards and debit card, Aadhar Enabled Payment System (AEPS), etc. Through there are arguments against this as digital transactions require use of cell phones for customers and point- of -sale (PoS) machines for merchants, which will only work if there is internet connectivity. On the contrary , these disadvantages are counterbalanced by an understanding that it helps people into the formal economy, thereby increasing financial saving and reducing tax evasion.

◆ IMPACT OF DEMONETISATION

1. **Money/ Interest rates:**

   (a)   Decline in cash transactions

   (b)   Bank deposits increased

   (c)   Increase in financial savings

   (d)   Interest rates decreased.

2. **Tax collection:**

   Rise in income tax collection because of increased disclosure.

3. **Digitisation:**

   Digital transactions amongst new users (RuPay/ AEPS) increased.

4. **Private and public sector wealth:**

    Private wealth declined since some high demonetised notes were not returned and real estate prices decline. However, there was no effect on public sector wealth.

◆ **Impact of government policy (for all three LPG)**

    1. Increasing competition

    2. More demanding customer

    3. Market orientation

    4. Rapidly changing technology

    5. Necessity for change

    6. Loss of budgetary support

Conclusion:- on the whole, the impact of government policy changes in respect of liberalisation, privatisation and globalisation has been positive as the Indian firms have developed strategies and adopted challenges.

▦ **Managerial response to change in business environment**

    1. Diversification spree

    2. Joint venture

    3. Brand building

    4. Use of latest technology

    5. Sharply improved compensation levels

    6. Customer focus

From Author- If you feel depressed -sing, feel sad-laugh, feel ill-double labour, feel inferior —wear new garments if you feel incompetent do Remember your past successes.
Success has no quota it comes from hard work and dedication.

PLANNING (4 to 8 marks)

Planning means deciding in advance what to do and how to do for successful achievement of organisational goal.

E.g.-target of Scoring 90% in class 12th exam

✄ STEPS IN PLANNING   (JOURNEY OF your Aim)

1.	**Setting objectives:–** Objectives, which specify what the organisation wants to achieve.
2.	**Developing premise:–** Make a certain assumptions about the future.
3.	**Identifying alternative course of action:-** Identify all possible alternative courses of action.
4.	**Evaluating alternative course of action:-** Positive and negative aspects of each alternative need to be evaluated.
5.	**Selecting an alternative:–** This is the real point of decision making. The best plan has to be adopted.
6.	**Implementing plan–** Putting the plan into action.
7.	**Follow up action–** Managers monitor the plan carefully to ensure that the premises are holding true in the present condition.

◆ **FEATURES OF PLANNING**

    a.   primary function of management

    b.   pervasive function

    c.   futuristic

    d.   mental exercise

    e.   continuous process

    f.   involve decision making

◆ **IMPORTANCE OF PLANNING (why to make plan)**

Q:- Failing to plan is planning to fail, explain this statement ?

1.   Provide direction

2.   Reduce risk of uncertainty

3.   Facilitate decision making

4.   Reduce overlapping and wasteful activities

5.   Promotes innovating ideas

6.   Establish standard for controlling

◆ **LIMITATION OF PLANNING (NCR KI DTC BEKAR HAI)**

1.   Leads to rigidity

2.   Reduce creativity

3.   Time consuming process

4.   Involve huge cost

5.   Not guarantee success

6.   Not work in dynamic environment

◆ **TYPES OF PLANS:-**

Single use plans- develop for one time event of project.

Eg. Budgets, Programer and project etc.

Standing plans- used for activities that occur regularly over a period of time.

Eg. Policies, procedures, methods and rules etc

✄ DIFFERENCE BETWEEN STANDING AND SINGLE- USE PLANS

BASIS OF DIFFER-ENCE	STANDING PLANS	SINGLE- USE PLANS
1. Period	These plans are formulated for a long period.	These plans are for a short period and are repeatedly formulated in case of need.
2. Object	These plans are formulated to bring about infirmity in the decisions.	These plans are designed to run successfully some particular activities.
3. Types	They are of six types: (i) Objectives, (ii) Strategies, (iii) Policies, (iv) Procedures, (v) Methods and (vi) Rules	They are of two types: (i) Budget and (ii) Programme
4. Scope	They guide the mangers in particular matters like price policy and sales policy.	These plans guide in matters of daily routine.

☞	They are designed to meet the demand of specific situations.	☞	They are designed to serve guidelines or criteria for the smooth functioning of the organisation.
☞	They are discarded when the situations are over.	☞	They remain relatively stable.
☞	Examples: Method, Programme, Budget, Etc.	☞	Examples: Objectives, Policy, Strategy, Procedure, Rule.

OBJECTIVES: (qualitative and quantitative)

Objectives are defined as ends which the management seeks to achieve by its operation. It should be measurable in quantitative terms.

e.g. - increasing sale by 10%

STRATEGY

A strategy is a long term plan for executing the idea into action. It is a comprehensive plan for accomplishing an organisation's goal.

Each deparment makes its strategy to achive organisational goal.

Eg. - Marketing strategy, finance strategy, pricing strategy, sales promotion technique.

(Mostly will be covered in marketing mgmt. chapter.)

POLICIES:

Policies are general statement or understanding which guide thinking in decision making.

e.g. - we don't sell on credit, no bargain, no exchange, cash on delivery.

PROCEDURE:

A procedure consists of sequential steps to carry out activities within policy framework to attain predetermined objectives.

e.g. - selection procedure of an employee.

RULE:

Rules are specifics statements that inform what is to be done. It does not allow for any flexibility or discretion.

e.g. - no smoking. NO parking

METHODS:

Methods are standardised ways or manner in which a task has to be performed considering the objectives.

e.g. - training methods of company.

(On the job, off the job)

PROGRAMMS:

Programs are the combination of goals, policies, procedures and rules about. All these plans together form programs.

e.g. - program for development of new product, opening of a new department.

Government program like SWACH BHARAT ABHIYAAN, BETI BACHAO BETI PADHAO

BUDGET:

A budget is a statement of expected results expressed in numerical terms for a definite period of time in the future.

e.g. - cash budget, production budget, sales budget etc.

✄ DIFFERENCE BETWEEN OBJECTIVES AND POLICY

OBJECTIVES	POLICY
☞ Objectives are defined as ends which the management seeks to achieve by its operations.	☞ Policies are general statements or understandings that guide or channel thinking in decision – making.
☞ They define the future state of affairs which the organisation would like to realise.	☞ They define the broad parameters within which a manager may function

☞ Examples: Increasing sales by 10% earning 20% ROI, etc.	☞ Examples: Selling products on cash basis only, insisting on fixed pricing, promoting from within the organisation, etc.

�֎ DIFFERENCE BETWEEN POLICY AND STRATEGY

POLICY	STARTEGY
☞ Policies are general statements that guide or channel thinking in decision-making. They define the broad parameters, within which a manager may function.	☞ A 'Strategy' refers to future decisions defining the organisation's direction and scope in the long run.
☞ There are policies for all levels, and departments. They are formulated to deal with repetitive problems.	☞ A 'Strategy' is a comprehensive plan which is formulated to counter environmental threats and capitalise on opportunities.
☞ Examples: Selling products on cash basis only, insisting on fixed pricing, promoting from within the organisation, etc.	☞ Examples: Choice of channels of distribution, pricing strategy, choice of advertising media, etc.

✖ DIFFERNCE BETWEEN POLICY AND PROCEDURE

POLICY	PROCEDURE
☞ Policies are general statements or understandings that guide or channel thinking in decision-making	☞ Procedure are sequence of routine steps on how to carry out activities. Procedures are guides to action, rather than to thinking.

☞	They define the broad parameters within which a manger may function.	☞	The detail the exact manner in which any work is to be performed.
☞	There are policies for all levels and departments. Company's competitors, etc.	☞	Procedure are generally meant for insiders to follow
☞	Examples: Selling products on cash basis only, insisting on fixed pricing promoting from within the organisation, etc.	☞	Examples: include procedure for purchase of raw materials, processing of orders, selection of employees, redressal of grievances, holding and conducting meetings, etc.

✖ DIFFERENCE BETWEEN POLICY AND RULE

POLICY		RULE	
☞	Policies are general statements or understandings that guide or channel thinking in decision-making. They define the broad parameters within which a manager may function.	☞	Rules are specific statements that inform what is to be done. A 'rule' reflects a managerial decision that a certain action must or must not be taken.
☞	Example: Selling products on cash basis only, insisting on fixed pricing, promoting from within the organisation, etc.	☞	Example: rule of 'No smoking' inside the office premises.
☞	Policies are flexible.	☞	Rules are rigid.
☞	No fine or penalty specified.	☞	There is generally a fine or penalty for violation of rules.

✂ DIFFERENCE BETWEEN RULE AND METHOD

RULE	METHOD
☞ Rules are specific statements that inform what is to be done. A 'rule' reflects a managerial decision that a certain action must or must not be taken.	☞ Methods are standardised ways or manner in which a task has to be performed considering the objective.
☞ Example: Rule of 'No smoking' inside the office premises.	☞ Example: On the job training methods of training for supervisory management and lectures/ seminars for top management.
☞ Rules are rigid.	☞ Methods are flexible.
☞ There is generally a fine or penalty for violation of rules.	☞ No fine or penalty for violation.
☞ Rules ensure discipline in the organisation.	☞ Selection of proper method saves time, money and effort, and increase efficiency.

✂ DIFFERENCE BETWEEN METHOD AND BUDGET

Basis of difference	Methods	Budgets
1. **Meaning**	Methods are that plan which determines how different activities of the procedure are completed.	Budgets describe the desired results in numerical terms.
2. **Selection**	There may be many methods to do a particular work. After extensive study a most suitable method has to be selected.	It is an instrument of both planning and controlling hence no question of selection arises.

Basis of difference	Objective	Strategy
1. **Meaning**	An objective is the end towards which all activities of the organisation are directed.	A strategy is a comprehensive plan formulated to achieve an objective
2. **Main Element**	An objective needs to be expressed in measurable terms and is to be achieved within a given time period	The business environment needs to be taken into consideration whenever a strategy is formulated.

From Author- The best day-today, greatest sin-fear, best gift-forgiveness, greatest need-

Organizing is the process of defining and grouping the activities of the enterprises and establishing authority relationship among them.

e.g. - In bank cashier, enquiry, cash deposit all have different work in organized manner

◆ **Organizing process (IDA REPORT):-**

1. Identification of work –

Identifying and dividing the total work to be done into small and manageable activities

2. Departmentation –

Grouping similar/ related jobs into larger units called departments or divisions.

3. Assignment of duties –

Allocate work/ jobs to the members of each department in accordance with their skills and competencies.

4. Establishing reporting relationship –

Authority responsibility relationship is established so that each individual may know from whom he/ she has to take orders and to whom he/ she is accountable.

◆ **Features of organizing:-**

1. Division of work

2. Coordination

3. Plurality of persons

4. Common objectives

◆ **Importance of organizing:- (*SAD GOA*)**

1. Benefits of specialization

2. Clarity in working relationship

3. Effective administration

4. Optimum utilization of resources

5. Expansion and growth

6. Adaption to change

7. Development of personnel

ORGANISATIONAL STRUCTURE:

Organisation structure refers to the framework within which managerial and operating tasks are performed.

It specifies the relationship between people, work and resources.

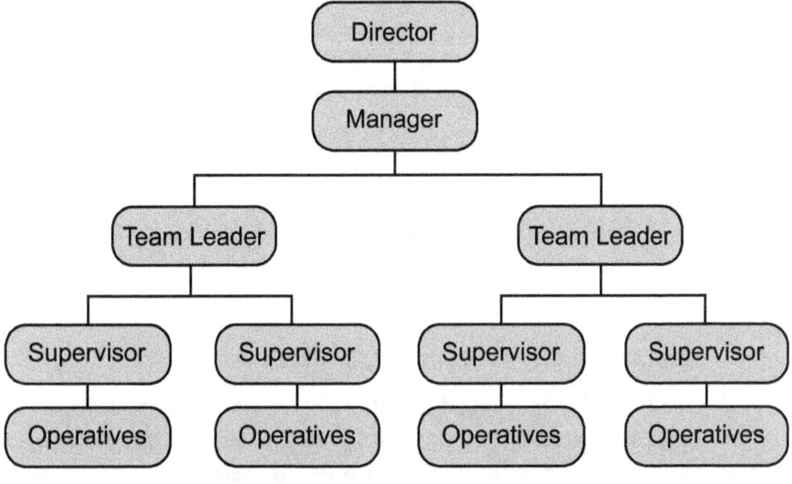

FORMAL ORGANISATION:

Formal organisation refers to the organisation structure which is designed by the management to achieve organisational goals.

The structure in a formal organisation can be functional or divisional.

Eg- Teaching methodology in school,

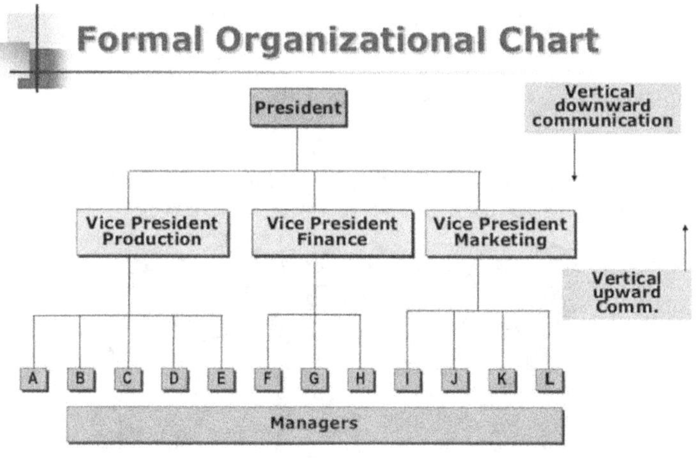

◆ **Features of Formal organisation:-**

1. Deliberately designed

2. Specify the relationship

3. Means to achieve the objectives

4. Communication through scalar chain

5. Standards of behaviors are laid down

✂ **Advantages and disadvantages of formal organisation:-**

ADVANTAGES	DISADVANTAGES
Easier to fix responsibility	Procedural delay (govt work)
Avoiding duplilication of efforts	Not provide adequate recognition to creative talent

Unity of command is maintained	Difficult to understand all human relationship
Effective accomplishment of goals	
Stability to the organisation	

INFORMAL ORGANISATION:

Interaction among people at work gives rise to a network of social relationship among employee" called informal organisation.

E.g.-Teaching methodology in coaching center // Managers playing cricket with subordinates.

◆ **Features of an informal organisation:-**

1.   Originates from personal interaction among employees

2.   Not deliberately created/emerge spontaneously

3.   Standards and behavior evolve from group norms

4.   Does not have fixed line of communication

5.   No definite structure or forms

✄ **Advantages and disadvantages of informal organisation:-**

ADVANTAGES	DISADVANTAGES
Faster speed	Spreads rumors

Fulfill social need	Resist any change in the organisation
Compensate inadequacies in the formal organisation	Pressurizes members to conform to group expectations.

✄ **Difference between formal organisation and Informal organisation:-**

Basis	Formal organisation	Informal organisation
Meaning	Structure of authority relationship created by the management	Network social relationship arising out of interaction among employees
Origin	Arises as a result of company rules and policies	Arises as a result of social interaction
Authority	Arises by virtue of position in management	Arises out of personal qualities
Behavior	It is directed by rules	There is no set behavior pattern
Flow of Communication	Communication takes place through the scalar chain	Flow of communication is not through a planned route. It can take place in any direction
Nature	Rigid	Flexible
Leadership	Managers are leaders.	Leaders may or may not be mangers. They are chosen by the group.

FUNCTIONAL STRUCTURE:

When the activities or jobs are grouped keeping in mind the functions or the job then it is called functional structure.

In a company there are HR manager, Marketing manager, Finance manager, Research manager, Production manager etc working as separate functions.

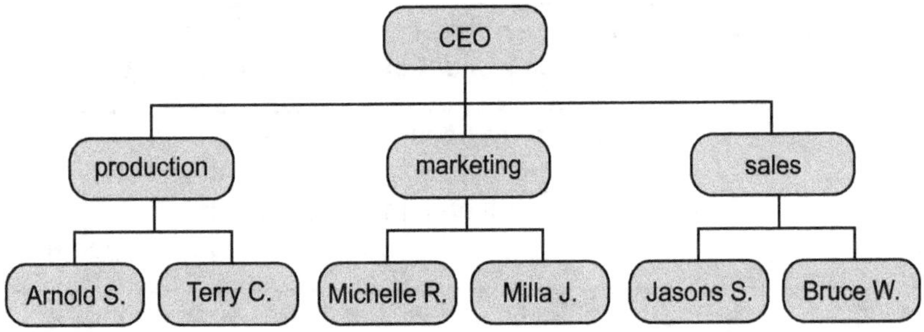

Advantage and Disadvantages of functional structure:-

ADVANTAGES	DISADVANTAGES
Functional specialization	Emphasis on departmental objectives
Increasing managerial and operational efficiency	Conflict of interest
Control and coordination within a department	Lead to inflexibility
Due attention	Difficult to fix responsibility
Training of employee easier	Managerial development is difficult
Minimum duplication of efforts	

Suitability:- suitable for <u>*medium sized*</u> firm having <u>*single product*</u> or small number or related product.

DIVISIONAL STRUCTURE:

When the organisation is large in size and is producing more than one type of product then activities related to one product are grouped under one department.

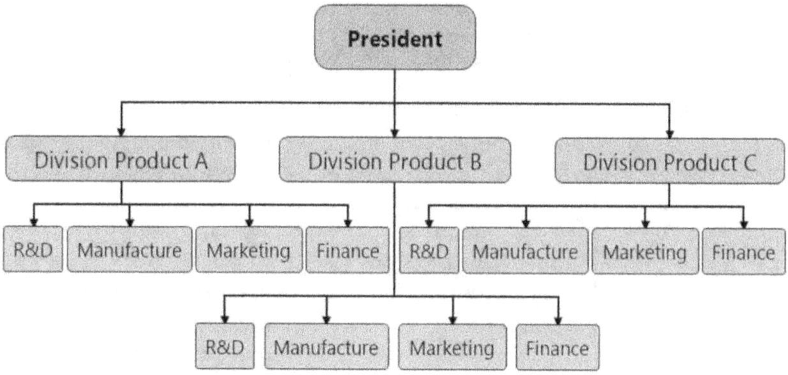

Advantage and Disadvantages of Divisional structure:-

ADVANTAGES	DISADVANTAGES
Help in development of varied skills	Conflict may arise among different divisions
Help in fixation of responsibility	Lead to increase in costs
Promotes flexibility and initiative	Ignore organisational interests
Facilitates growth and expansion	Organisational structure become complex
Managerial development is easy	
Coordination becomes easy	

Suitability:- suitable for *large* firm having *multiple products with distinctive characteristics*.

✄ **Difference between functional and divisional structure:-**

Basis	Functional Structure	Divisional Structure
Formation	Formation is based on functions	Formation is based on product lines and is supported by functions.
Specialization	Functional specialization	Product specialization.
Responsibility	Difficult to fix on a department.	Easy to fix responsibility for performance.
Managerial Development	Difficult, as each functional manager has to report to the top management.	Easier, autonomy as well as the chance to perform multiple functions helps in managerial development.
Cost	Functions are not duplicated hence economical	Duplication of resources in various departments, hence costly.
Coordination	Difficult for a multiproduct company.	Easy, because all functions related to a particular product are integrated in one department.

DELEGATION:

Delegation refers to the downward transfer of authority from a superior to a subordinate.

Delegation of authority is based on the elementary principals of division work.

e.g.: - physics teacher teaching maths in the absence of maths teacher.

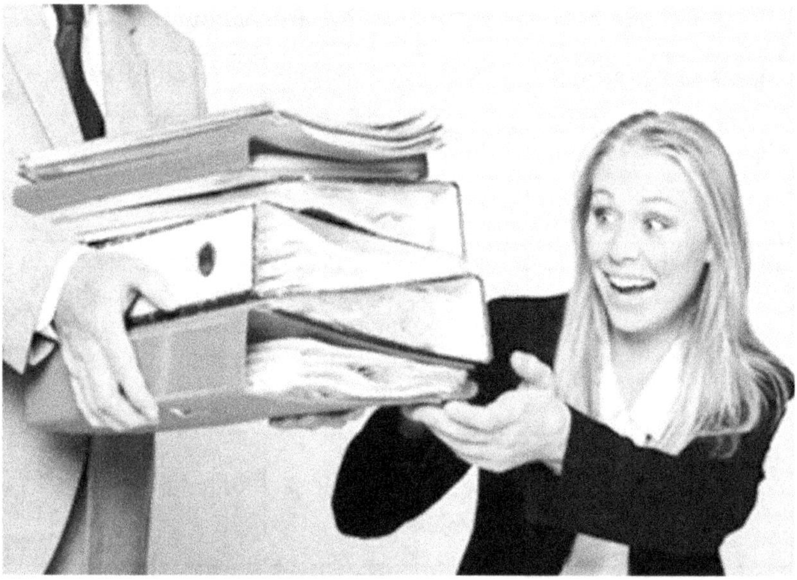

◆ **Principal of delegation:-**

1. Authority granted must be equal to the responsibility assigned
2. Delegation does not mean abdication
3. Authority granted to a subordinate can be taken back and re-delegated to another person.

Elements of Delegation:-

AUTHORITY	RESPONSIBILTY	ACCOUNTABILTY
It refers to right of an individual to command his subordinate and to take action within the scope of his/her position.	It refers to obligation of a subordinate to properly perform the assigned duty.	It refers to answerability for the final outcome of the assigned task.
Flow from top to bottom	It flows upward	Flows upward. It cannot be elegated

✁ Difference between responsibility and accountability

Basis of Difference	Responsibility	Accountability
(i) Meaning	The assigned job.	Answerable to the superior for the work performed.
(ii) Delegation	Responsibility (Responsibility for) or the work can be delegated to some other person.	Accountability (Responsibility to) cannot be delegated to some other person.
(iii) Origin	Relationship between senior and subordinate.	Delegation of Authority.

◆ **Importance of Delegation:-**

1. Effective management
2. Motivation of employee
3. Employee development
4. Facilitation of growth
5. Better coordination
6. Creation of management hierarchy

◆ **Centralization and Decentralization**

DECENTRALISATION:

Decentralization refers to systematic delegation of authority through all the level of management and in all departments of the organisation.

Decision making authority is shared with lower level of management.

Eg:-banking working system

☞ When we delegate authority, we multiply it by two. When we de-centralize authority, we multiply it by many.

◆ **Importance of Decentralization**

1. Relief to top management

2. Develops initiative amongst subordinates

3. Develops managerial talent for the future

4. Facilitate growth

5. Quick decision

6. Better control

✂ **Distinguish between 'Delegation' and 'Decentralisation'**

BASIS OF DIFFERENCE	DELEGATION OF AUTHORITY	DECENTRALISATION
1. **Purpose**	The purpose is reduction of the workload of an officer.	The purpose is expansion of the authority in an organisation.

2.	Scope	Delegation of Authority depicts limited distribution of authority that is why its scope is limited.	This depicts broader distribution of authority that is why its scope is broad.
3.	Status	This is a process done as a result of division of work.	This is a result of the policies framed by higher officials.
4.	Nature	Delegation of authority is inevitable for every organisation because mangers have to delegate authority to their subordinates in order to get the work done. Thus, work cannot proceed in its absence.	It is not necessary to be found in every organisation because it is not essential that senior officers distribute their authority throughout the organisation. Thus, work can proceed in its absence.

CENTRALISATION:

Centralization means concentration of all decision making function at the apex of management hierarchy.

e.g.: - MAC.D and BATA showroom price

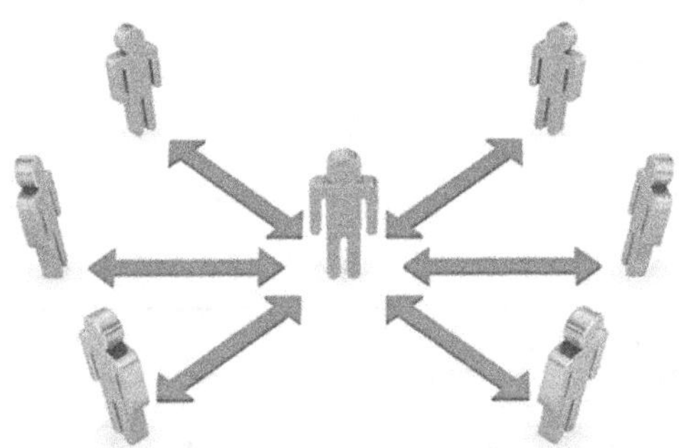

From Author- Character should be your degree, life should be your examination, and universe is your university, so as a student STAY HUNGRY STAY FOOLISH.

Staffing is the managerial functions of filling and keeping filled positions in the organisation.

It means putting right person at right place in right time at right cost. It is the function of human resource manager.

◆ **Importance of staffing:-**

1. Obtaining competent personnel

2. Higher performance

3. Continuous survival and growth

4. Optimum utilization of human resources

5. Improves job satisfaction and morals of employees

◆ **Staffing process**

1. Estimating manpower requirement

    (a) **Workload analysis:-** assessment of the number and types of human resource necessary for the performance of various jobs

    (b) **Workforce analysis:-** it estimates the number and types of human resource available.

2. Recruitment

3. Selection

4. Placement and orientation

5. Training and development

6. Performance appraisal

7. Promotion and career planning

8. Compensation

RECRUITMENT:

Recruitment is the process of searching for prospective employees and stimulating them to apply for jobs in the organisation.

It is the positive process which aims at attracting a number of candidates to apply for the given job.

e.g.: - vacancy in newspaper and pamphlet in locality.

◆ **Recruitment process-**

(a) Identification of different sources of recruitment, e.g. , advertisement, employment exchanges, management consultants, internal promotions, etc.

(b) Assessment of their validity;

(c) Choosing the most suitable sources; and

(d) Inviting applications from the prospective candidates for the vacancies.

Internal source	External source
It refers to inviting candidates from within the organisation.	It refers to inviting candidates from outside the organisation.
1. Transfer	1. Campus recruitment
2. Promotion	2. Advertisement
3. Lay off	4. Direct recruitment (website or gate)
	5. Casual caller
	6. Recommendation of employee
	7. Web publishing (shine.com, naukri.com, moster.com, etc)
	8. Employment exchange (government job)
	9. Management consultant
	10. Labour contractor

Internal source of Recruitment:

◆ **Merits;-**

1. Economical source

2. Motivates employee

3. Simple process

4. Adjust of surplus (by transfer and promotion)

5. No need of training

6. Peace prevail

◆ **Limitation**

    1.   Incomplete source

2. Employee may become lethargic

3. Spirit of completion hampered

4. Reduce productivity

5. New enterprise cannot use internal sources

6. Limited choice

External source of Recruitment

◆ **Merits;-**

1. Qualified personnel

2. Wider choice

3. Fresh talent

4. Competitive spirit

◆ **Limitation**

1. Dissatisfaction among existing employee

2. costly

3. lengthy process

SELECTION:

Selection is the process identifying and choosing the best person out of number of prospective candidates who have applied for a job.

Selection is a negative process.

e.g.: - in Delhi university students are selected based on their merit list.

◆ **Selection process:-**

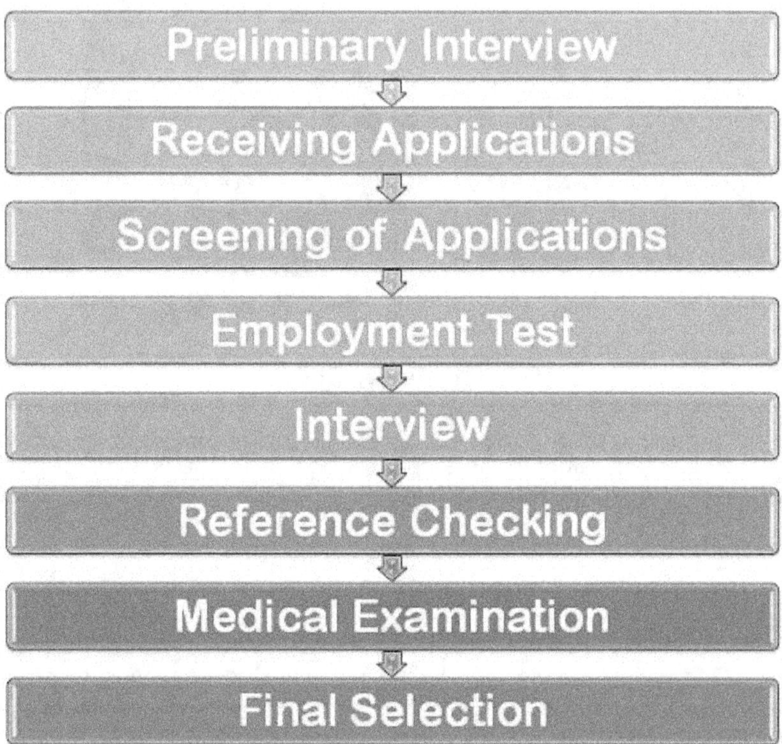

1. Preliminary screening
2. Selection test
   a. Trade test
   b. Personality test
   c. Aptitude test
3. Employment interview
4. Reference and background check
5. Selection decision
6. Medical examination (in selected job)
7. Job offer
8. Contract of employment

PLACEMENT:

Placement refers to the employee occupying the position or post for which he\she has been selected.

ORIENTATION:

Orientation means introducing the selected employee to other employees and familiarising him\her with the rules and policies of the organisation.

e.g.: - new student's introduction by teacher with all existing students...

Training refers to the process by which the aptitudes, skills and abilities of employees to perform specific jobs are improved.

Development refers to the process by which the employees acquire skills and competencies for handling higher jobs in future.

Methods of Training

a.   On the job Training (new book for more types)

1.   Apprenticeship training (plumber, electricians etc)

2.   Internship training (CA,MBBS,LAW)

3.   Induction training (introducing with new and familiarize)

4.   Job Rotation

b.   Off the job Training

1.   Vestibule training (identical machine)

2.   Conference (refer book)

3.   Seminars (refer book)

4.   Film

5.   Case study

6.   Computer modeling

c.   Other methods of training

1. Coaching

2. Classroom lectures/ conferences

3. Programmed instruction

✄   **ON THE JOB AND OFF THE JOB TRAINING METHOD**

On The Job Methods	Off The Job Methods
☞ On the job methods refer to the methods that are applied to the workplace, while the employee is actually working.	☞ Off the job methods are used away from the work place. It means – "learning before doing." Examples: Vestibule training,

It means- "learning while doing". Examples: Apprenticeship training, internship tainting, job rotation, coaching, etc.	lectures/ conferences, films, case study, etc.
☞ Training is provided by superiors to subordinates.	☞ Training is provided by experts from within or outside the organisation.
☞ It is less costly.	☞ It is more costly.
☞ It is less time consuming.	☞ It is more time consuming.
☞ It is used where jobs are simple, as in case of plumbers or iron workers.	☞ It is used where jobs are complex involving the use of sophisticated machinery and equipment.

✄ IMPORTANCE OF TRAINING AND DEVELOPMENT

To The Organisation / Company	To The Employees
Avoid wastage of efforts and money	Promotion and career growth
Higher profits	Helps them to earn more
Equips future managers	More efficient to handle machines
Reduces absenteeism and employee turnover	Increases the satisfaction and morale
Effective response to a fast changing environment	Better employment opportunities

✄ DIFFERENCE BETWEEN TRAINING AND DEVELOPMENT

Basis	Training	Development
meaning	It is a process of increasing knowledge and skills.	It is a process of learning and growth.

purpose	It is to enable the employee to do the job better.	It is to enable the overall growth of the employee.
Job or career	It is a job oriented process.	It is a career oriented process.
Scope	limited	Broad. Training is part of development

◆ HUMAN RESOURCE MANAGEMENT

HRM is a much broader concept and staffing is an inherent part of it.

It includes duties of recruitment, analyzing jobs, developing compensation and incentive plans, training and development of employees, maintaining laour relation, handling grievances and complaints, providing for social security and welfare of employees, We can say that staffing is an inherent part of HRM.

◆ Human Resource Management includes many specified activities and duties which the human resource personnel must perform. These duties are:

- ✔ Recruitment i.e. search for qualified people.
- ✔ Analyzing jobs collecting information about jobs to prepare job descriptions.
- ✔ Developing compensation and incentive plans.
- ✔ Training and development of employees for efficient performance and career growth.
- ✔ Maintaining labour relations and union management relations.
- ✔ Handling grievances and complaints.
- ✔ Providing for social security and welfare of employees.
- ✔ Defending the company in law suits and avoiding legal complications.

From Author- Stand up, be bold, be strong. Take the whole responsibility on your own shoulders and know that you are creator of your own destiny.

DIRECTING (5 to 8marks)

Directing as a function of the management refers to the process of instructing, guiding, counseling, motivating and leading people in the organisation to achieve its objectives.

Directing is the key element of the management process.

Eg: - a director of a movie direct to act in a particular situation/scene.

◆ **Features of Directing:-**

1. Directing initiate action

2. Directing takes place in every level of management

3. Continuous process

4. Directing flows from top to bottom

◆ **Importance of Directing:-**

1. Initiate action

2. Integrate employee efforts

3. Guides employee

4. Facilitates introduction of changes

5. Bring stability and balance

◆ **Principles of Directing**

1. Harmony of objectives
2. Unity of command
3. Appropriateness of direction
4. Democratic leadership
5. Managerial communication
6. Follow through
7. Maximum individual contribution
8. Strategic use of informal organisation

✄ **Elements of Directing**

Supervision	Motivation	Leadership	Communication

SUPERVISION:

The word supervision is formed by joining two words 'super' and 'vision'.

It means "overseeing what is being done by subordinates and giving instructions to ensure optimum utilization of resources and achievement of work targets.

e.g.:-examiner in exam hall supervises all.

✕ **Distinguish between 'Direction' and 'Supervision'.**

Basis of Direction	Direction	Supervision
(1) Meaning	It refers to instructing, guiding, communicating and inspiring people so that the objective can be achieved.	It refers to monitoring the progress of work of one's subordinates and guiding them properly.
(2) Scope	Its scope is wider as supervisions is one of the elements of it.	Its scope is narrower as it is one of the elements of direction.

◆ **Role of supervisor:-**

1. Act as a key man

2. Act as a mediator

3. Act as a human relation specialist

◆ **Functions performed by Supervisor**

a. Maintain day to day contact

b. Ensure performance of work

c. Gives feedback

d. Link between worker and management

e. Provide on the job training

f. Help in maintaining group unity

MOTIVATION:

Motivation means the process of stimulating people to action to accomplish desired goals.

Or

It refers to that process which excites people to work for the attainment of a desired objective.

◆ Features of motivation

1. It is an internal feeling
2. Goal directed behavior
3. Can be positive and negative
4. Complex process

◆ Importance of motivation

1. Motivation sets in motion the action of people and ensures achievement of organisational goals
2. Improves performance levels of employees
3. Reduction in resistance to change
4. Reduction in employees turnover and turnover and absenteeism in the organisation
5. Positive attitude of employees
6. Supportive work environment
7. Better utilization of resources

MOTIVATION PROCESS (how an employee can get motivated)

Unsatisfied need – tension – drives – search behavior – satisfied need

An employee has a need for promotion to higher position. (Unsatisfied need), if this need is strong, it creates tension to the employee which stimulates his or her drives. These drive generate a search behaviour to satisfy such need. If such need is satisfied, the indivisual is relieved of Tension.

Eg:- Need of food.

MASHOW HIRARCHY THEORY OF MOTIVATION.........

1.	Basic needs (giving basic salary)
2.	Safety needs (job security, stability of income)
3.	Social needs (informal relations among employee)
4.	Esteem needs (giving job title and recognition)
5.	Self actualization needs (allowing the employee to take initiative to become what they are capable of becoming)

Self Actualization needs (Growth and self fulfillment)
Esteem needs (Self respect autonomy status ect.)
Affiliation/ Belongingness needs (Affection acceptance sense of belongingness etc)
Safety/ security needs (Protection against dangers safety of property etc)

Basic physiological needs

(Hunger thirst shelter and sleep)

◆ **Assumption of Maslow's theory:-**

1. Behavior being affected by their needs.

2. Needs of people must be in order or priority can be made.

3. Motivation ends with the satisfaction of needs.

4. People move to next higher need only when lower level needs are satisfied.

INCENTIVES:

Incentives means all measure (monetary and non monetary) which are used to motivate people to improve performance.

◆ **Financial and non-financial Incentives**

Financial Incentives:

Benefits payable to employee which can be measured in terms of money.

◆ **Examples of financial incentive:-**

1. Pay and allowances(HRA, DA, CA)
2. Profit sharing
3. Bonus
4. Retirement benefits (Pension, Gratuity)
5. Perquisites (Car, Medical, House)
6. Stock option/ co-partnership (Share of Company)

Non-Financial Incentives:

Incentives which cannot be measured in terms of money but provide psychological and emotional satisfaction to the employee.

◆ **Example of non financial incentives (C-ROSE)**

1. job security (stability of future income)
2. status (managerial position)
3. recognition (appreciation for good work)

4. career advancement opportunities (skill development programs)

5. employee participation (in decision making)

6. employee empowerment (giving power or autonomy)

7. organisational climate (Rules, policy)

8. job enrichment (Promotion chances)

✼ **Difference between financial and non financial incentives:-**

Basis	Financial incentives	Non-financial incentives
Meaning	Direct monetary form or measurable in terms of money.	Not measured in terms of money but provide psychological and emotional satisfaction to employee.
Level of employee	Suitable for lower level of employee	More suitable for higher level of employee.
Need satisfied	Satisfy basic physiological needs of employee.	Satisfy, social and esteem needs of the employee.

LEADERSHIP:

It is the process of influencing the behavior of people at work towards the achievement of organisational goal.

Or

It refers to influencing others in such a manner to do what the leader wants them to do.

e.g.:-Dhirubhai Ambani (reliance), narayan murthy (Infosys), J.R.D. Tata (TATA), dhoni for team India etc. are some of the example of great leader.

◆ Features of Leadership

1. Influencing process
2. Behavior changing process
3. Interpersonal relations between leader and followers
4. Achieves common goals
5. Continuous process

◆ Importance of leadership

1. Helps in guiding and inspiring employees
2. Secures cooperation of members of organisation
3. Create confidence
4. Improves productivity
5. Improves job satisfaction
6. Achievement of organisational goal
7. Introducing required changes
8. Handles conflict effectively
9. Provide training

◆ Qualities of a good leader

1. Physical features
2. Knowledge
3. Integrity

4. Initiative

5. Communication skills

6. Motivation skills

7. Self confidence

8. Decisiveness

9. Social skills

�֎ MANAGERSHIP AND LEADERSHIP:-

BASIS OF DIFFERENCE	MANAGERSHIP	LEADERSHIP
1. Basis of Existence	Organised group or formal organisation	Unorganised group or informal organisation
2. Focus	Attainment of the objectives of the organisation	To satisfy the expectations and aspirations of the followers.
3. Authority	Formal authority	Informal authority- the followers themselves allow the leader the authority to give orders and lead them
4. Scope	Widespread (It includes all the managerial activities.)	Limited (It is only a part of management.)

Manager +leadership ability=success

◆ **Leadership Style:-**

AUTOCRATIC OR AUTHORITARIAN LEADERSHIP

An autocratic leader gives order and insist that they are obeyed. He determines the policies for the group without consulting them.

This style is also known as the leader-centered style

- ### Advantages

    1. Effective in getting productivity

    2. Quick decision making

    3. Satisfactory work

    4. Necessary for less educated employees

- ### Characteristics

    a. Centralized authority

    b. Single man decision

    c. Wrong belief regarding employees

    d. Only downward communication

- ### Disadvantages

    1. Lack of motivation

    2. Agnation by employee

    3. Possibility of partiality

- ◆ **Suitability-**

    1. Where leader is knowledgeable

    2. Time is short for decision making

    3. Subordinate is uneducated

    4. Subordinate are inexperienced.

PARTICIPATIVE OR DEMOCRATIC LEADERSHIP:

A democratic leader gives order only after consulting the group and work out the polies with the acceptance of the group.

Also known as group-centered leadership style.

- ◆ **Advantages**

    1. Improve attitude of employee towards job

    2. Using this style is of mutual benefit

3. High morale

4. Create more efficiency

♦   **Features**

1. Cooperative relations

2. Belief in employees

3. Open communication

♦   **Disadvantages**

1. Requirement of educated subordinate

2. Delay in decision

3. Lack of responsibility in managers

♦   **Suitability-**

1. When group members are skilled

2. When plenty of time is available

3. Leader want involvement of subordinate in decision making.

FREE REIN OR LAISSEZ FAIRE LEADERSHIP:

A free rein leader gives complete freedom to the subordinates. Such a leader avoids use of power. It means no interference in the activities of subordinates.

♦   **Advantages**

1. Development of self-confidence in subordinate

2. High level motivation

3. Helpful in development and extension of the enterprise.

◆ **Disadvantages**

1. Difficulty in cooperation

2. Lack of importance of managerial post

3. Suitable only for highly educated employees

◆ **Suitability**

1. When followers are highly skilled

2. When followers have pride in their work

3. Followers are trustworthy

✄ **Comparison Between Leadership Styles**

Basis	Authoritative Style	Democratic Style	Laissez-faire Style
1. Decision – making	Leader takes all decisions alone without consulting subordinates; 'I' style.	Leader consults subordinates on proposed actions and decisions; 'We' style.	Subordinates themselves take decisions; 'You' style.
2. Motivation techniques	Threats and punishment.	Rewards and involvement	Self – direction and self – control.
3. Focus	Boss – centered leadership.	Group-centered leadership	Subordinates-centered leadership.
4. Delegation of authority	Complete control and supervision; no delegation of authority.	Delegation of authority.	Complete delegation of authority.

5. **Opportuni-ty to subor-dinates**	No scope for initiative and self-develop-ment.	Scope for initiative and self-development.	Full scope for initiative and self-development.
6. **Role of leader**	Strict manager, who commands and expects compliance.	Team manager, who operates according to majority opinion.	Contract person, who brings information and resources needed by subordinates to achieve group goals.
7. **Communi-cation**	One way (downward) communica-tion.	Two way (downward and upward) com-munication.	Free flow of communication

COMMUNICATION:

Communication is the process of exchange of information ideas and thoughts between two or more. Persons to reach common understanding.

Communication plays a key role in the success of managers.

◆ **Characteristics of communication**

1. Two or more person

2. Exchange of ideas

3. Mutual understanding

4. Direct and indirect communication

5. Continuous process

6. Use of words as well as symbols

◆ **Importance of communication**

1. Gains commitment of employees to organisational objectives

2. Provides data necessary for decision making

3. Classifies task responsibilities and authority positions

4. Facilitates coordination

5. Boosts morale and provides motivation

6. Smooth working of enterprise

7. Increases managerial efficiency

8. Promotes cooperation and industrial peace

COMMUNICATION PROCESS:

✄ **Element involve in communication process:-**

Sender
Message
Encoding
Media
Decoding
Receiver
Feedback
Noise (everywhere)

✄ **Classification of communication taking place in the organi-sation:-**

FORMAL COMMUNICATION	INFORMAL COMMUNICATION

FORMAL COMMUNICATION:

Formal communication refers to official communication which takes place following the channel designed in the organisation.

e.g.:- submission of progress report, sending notice of meeting.

◆ **Characteristics**

1. Written and oral
2. Formal communication
3. Prescbied path
4. Organized message
5. Deliberate efforts

Advantage and Disadvantage;-

ADVANTAGE	DISADVANTAGE
Maintenance of authority	Overload of work
Clear and effective communication	Distortion of information
Orderly flow of information	Indifferent officers
Easy flow of source of information	

FORMAL COMMUNICATION- MERITS AND LIMITATIONS

S. NO.	MERITS	LIMITATIONS
1.	The officially prescribed path of communication is orderly in nature. It can easily be maintained because it derives support from authority relationships.	Formal communication tends to be slow as it has to follow the path laid down by the management.
2.	It helps in exercising control over subordinates and in fixation of responsibility.	It is rigid as deviations are not allowed.
3.	Formal communication is authentic.	formal communication is impersonal
4.	Chances of distortion of information are very few.	

- **Classification of formal communication**

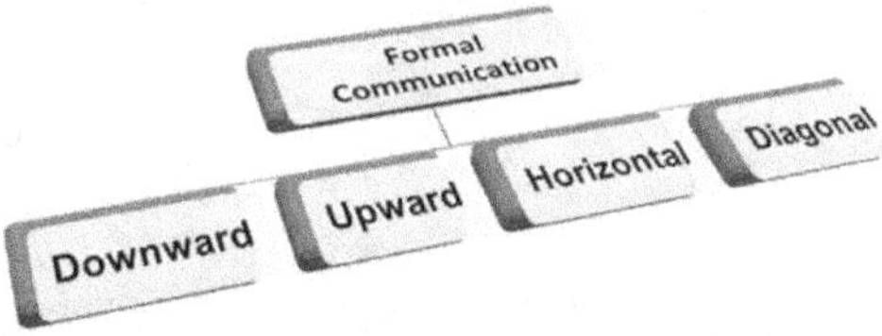

1. Vertical communication

2. Downward communication

3. Upward communication

4. Horizontal communication

◆   **Formal communication network**

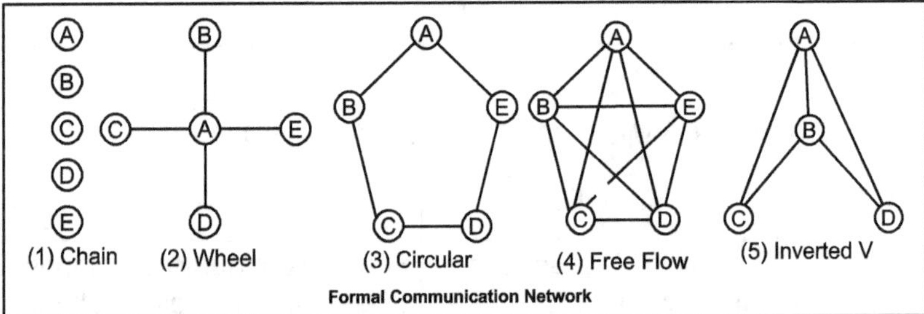

1. Single chain network

2. Wheel network

3. Circular network

4. Free flow network

5. Inverted V network

INFORMAL COMMUNICATION: (Grapevine channel of communication)

Communication which takes place without following the formal lines of communication. (Disregarding the level of authority.)

It takes place without following the formal lines of communication.

Eg:-talk with family members at home, Cafetaria Communication.

✄ Merits and limitation of informal communication:-

S. No.	Merits'	Demerits
1	Carry information rapidly	As information spreads rapidly so sometime distorted
2	Getting quick feedback	Generate gossips and rumours
3	Help to clarify official message	Information may hamper work environment

◆ **Informal communication network (also called grapevine network)**

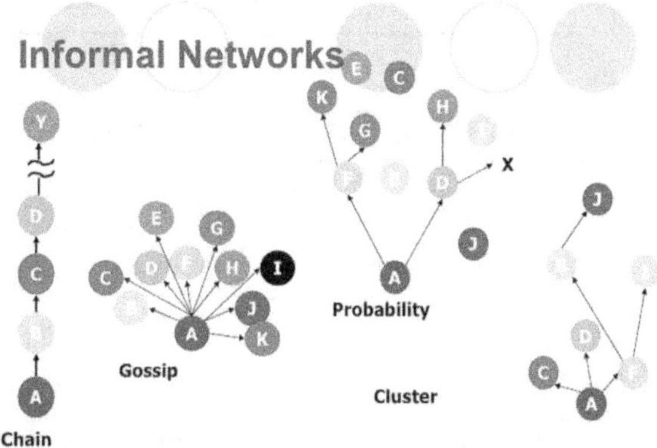

1. Single strand network

2. Gossip network

3. Probability network

4. Cluster network

✄ **Difference between formal and informal channel of communication:-**

Basis	Formal communication	Informal communication
Meaning	Communication which flow through official channel.	Communication take place without following the formal lines of communication
Direction of flow	Upward, downward, horizontal	Spread throughout the organisation with its branches
Form	Oral or written	Oral
Speed	Slow-time consuming	Fast-spread information rapidly
Authenticity (reliability)	Authentic information	Not authentic- generate rumors
Purpose	To achieve organisational objective	To meet personal or social needs of employee.

BARRIERS TO EFFECTIVCE COMMUNICATION:

- PYHISICAL BARRIERS
- ORGANISATIONAL BARRIERS
- CULTURAL BARRIERS
- LANGUAGE BARRIERS
- CHANNEL BARRIERS
- INTERPERSONAL BARRIERS
- INDIVIDUAL BARRIERS
- ATTITUDINAL BARRIERS
- LISTENING BARRIERS
- BARRIERS WHILE SPEAKING

A. Semantic barriers	B. Psychological barriers	C. Organisation barriers	D. Personal barriers
(word, grammar, encoding, decoding, symbol)	(mentally disturbance)	(policy and rule of organisation is not good)	(employee personal problems)
1. Badly expressed message	1. Lack of attention	1. Organisation policy	1. Fear of challenge of authority
2. Symbol with different meaning	2. Distrust	2. Rules and regulation	2. Lack of confidence of superior on his subordinate
3. Faulty translation	3. Premature evaluation	3. Organisational facilities	4. Lack of proper incentives

4. Unclarified assumption	4. Loss by transmission or poor retention	4. status	5. unwillingness to communicate
5. Technical Jargon		5. Complexity in organisation	
6. Body language			

◆ **Measures to improve communication effectiveness:-**

1. Clarify the ideas before communication
2. Communication according to the needs of receiver
3. Be aware of language tone and content of message
4. Be a good listener
5. Ensure proper feedback
6. Communicate for present as well as future.

From Author- Learning gives creativity, creativity leads to thinking. Thinking provides knowledge, knowledge makes you great.

CONTROLLING: (2 to marks)

Controlling means ensuring that activities in an organisation are performed as per the plans. It also ensure that an organisation's resources are being used effectively and efficiently for the achievement of predetermined goals.

◆ **Nature of controlling:-**

1. Controlling is a goal oriented function

2. Controlling is a pervasive function

3. Controlling is both backward and forward looking function

4. Controlling is a continuous process

CONTRLLING PROCESS (Roadmap of success):

1. Setting performance standards (qualitative and quantitive)

2. Measurement of actual performance

3. Comparing actual performance with standards

4. Analyzing deviations

    (a) Critical point control –focus on key result area

    (b) Management by exception-set a tolerance level

5. Taking corrective action

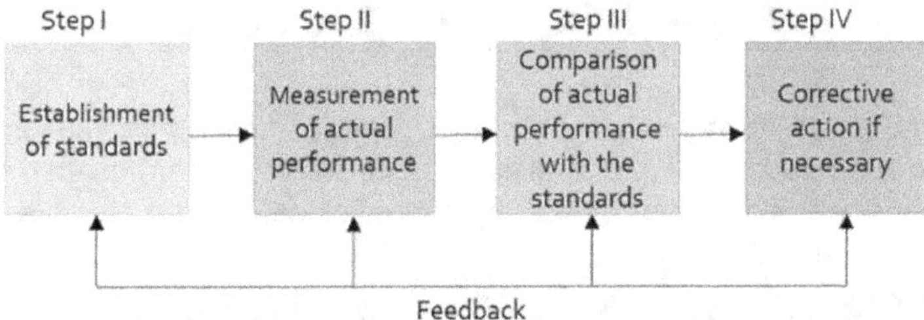

◆ CPC and MBE in detail

Critical Point Control (CPC): It helps in controlling process by focusing on key result areas (KRAs)

which are critical to the success of an organisation the key result areas are set as critical points since it is neither economical nor easy to keep a check on each and every activity in an organisation. If anything goes organisation suffers. For example, in a manufacturing organisation, an increase of 10

Per cent in the labour cost may be more troublesome than a 20 per cent increase in postal charges.

Advantages of CPC and MBE:

(i) It identifies critical problems which need timely action to keep the organisation in right track.

(ii) The routine problems are left to the subordinates. Management by exception, thus, facilities delegation of authority and increases morale of the employees.

(iii) It saves the time and efforts of managers as they deal with only significant deviations.

(iv) It focuses managerial attention on important areas. Thus, there is better utilisation of managerial talent.

◆ **Management by exception (MBE):** It means that "an attempt to control everything results in controlling nothing." It helps in the controlling process by identifying only significant deviations which cross the permissible limit/ acceptable range and bringing them to the notice of the management. Deviations within the acceptable range (i.e., minor deviations) are ignored.

IMPORTACNE OF COTROLLING:

1. Accomplishing organisational goal
2. Judging accuracy of standards
3. Efficient use of resources
4. Ensure order and discipline
5. Improving employees motivation and morale
6. Facilitate coordination of action

RELATIONSHIP BETWEEN PLANNING AND CONTROLLING:

1. No planning without controlling
2. No controlling without planning
3. Both planning and controlling are forward looking (for future)
4. Both planning and controlling are backward looking (to check past)
5. Both are the primary functions of management

LIMITATION OF CONTROLLING:

- Difficulty in setting quantitative standards
- No control on external factors
- Resistance from employee
- Costly affairs

TECHNIQUES OF MANAGERIAL CONTROL:

1. **Traditional techniques**

   (b) Personal observation

(c)   Statistical reports

(d)   Breakeven analysis

(e)   Budgetary control

1.   **Modern techniques**

(a)   Return on investment

(b)   Ratio analysis

(c)   Responsibility accounting

(d)   Management audit

(e)   PERT and CPM

(f)   Management information system

✂ KEY TERMS

Standards: Criteria against which actual performance would be measured.

Deviation: It is the difference between actual performance and standard performance.

Management by Exception (MBE): Only significant deviations which cross the

permissible limit should be brought to the notice of management.

Critical Point Control: Control technique should focus on the key result areas which are critical to the success of an organisation.

Feedback: A good control system must report the deviations quickly so that corrective

◆   **Types of Budgets**

1.   Sales Budget :

2.   Production Budget :

3.   Material Budget :

4.   Cash Budget :

5.   Capital Budget :

6.   Research and Development Budget :

◆ **Advantages of Budgetary Control**

1.   Attainment of organisational objectives :

2.   Motivation to the employees :

3.   Optimum utilization of resources :

4.   Achieving coordination among different departments :

5.   Facilitates management by exception :

FINANCIAL MANAGEMENT: (5 to 8 marks) [one of the field of management MBA]

Financial management is concerned with optimum procurement as well as usage of fund.

Financial management may be defined as planning, organizing, directing and controlling the financial activities of an organisation.

The primary objective of financial management is to maximize shareholder's wealth.

Finance is the life blood of business. Never invest your money in anything that eats or needs repairing

◆ Objective of financial management

1. Primary objective is maximization of shareholders wealth. This is possible if following ways:-

2. Ensuring availability of sufficient funds at reasonable cost

3. Ensuring effective utilization of funds

4. Ensuring safety of funds

FINANCIAL PLANING:

The process of estimating the funds requirement of a business and determining the sources of funds is called **"financial planning"**.

◆ **Importance of financial planning**

1. It helps the company to prepare for the future

2. Avoiding business shocks and surprise

3. Link between investment and financing decisions

4. Serve as a control technique

5. Developing a sound capital structure

6. Help to tackle the uncertainty

◆ **Process of financial planning**

a. Determination of financial objectives

b. Determination of financial policies

c. Determination of financial procedure

It is concerned with three broad decisions:-

1.   Investment decision

2.   Financing decision

3.   Dividend decision

◆   **Financial decisions**

The finance functions concerned with three broad decisions:-

Financing decision (paise kaha se laaye)	Investment decision (paisa kaha lagaye)	Dividend decision (profit baante ya nahi, how much.)

◆   **1.   Financing decision**

It relates to the quantum of finance to be raised from various long term sources.

Different Sources of funds are equity, debt (loan), retained earnings.

- ### Factor affecting financial decision

    1. Cash flow position of the company

    2. Cost

    3. Risk

    4. Level of fixed operating costs

    5. Floatation cost

    6. Control consideration

    7. State of the capital market / stock market condition

    8. Tax rate

- ### Investment decision

    Investment decision is concerned with how firm funds will be deploys in different alternatives (assets) to get maximum benefit (return)

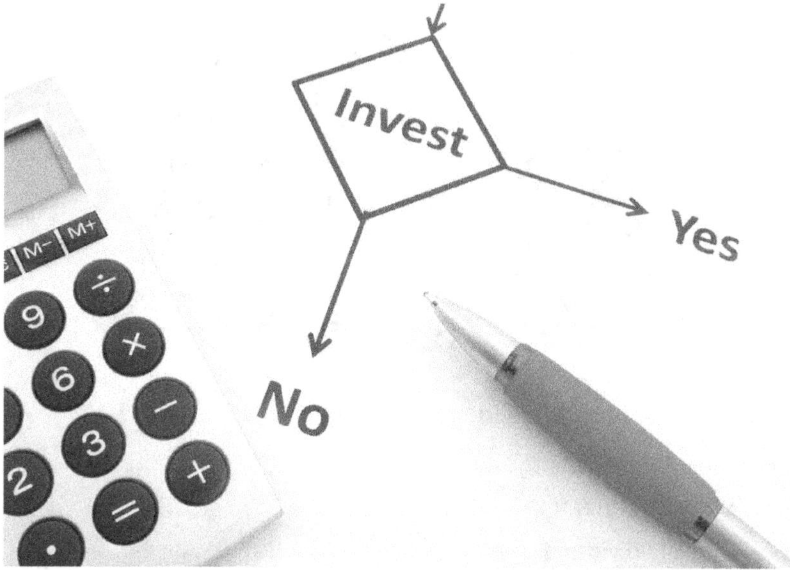

    Investment decision can be short term and long term. Long term investment decision is also called "capital budgeting decision".

    Short term investment decision is also called "working capital decision"

◆ **Factor affecting investment decision:-**

1. Rate of return of the project
2. Cash flow of the project
3. Investment criteria involved (NPV, IRR, PBP,ARR etc)
4. Risk

◆ **Dividend decision**

It relates to how much of the profit earned by the company is to be distributed to the shareholders as dividend and how much of it should be retained in the business.

◆ **Factor affecting dividend decision:-**

1. Amount of earning
2. Stability of earning
3. Stability dividend
4. Growth opportunities
5. Cash flow position
6. Share holder's preference
7. Taxation policy (DDT to pay)

8. Stock market reaction

9. Legal constraints

BUSINESS FINANCE:

Money required to carrying out business activities is called business finance. Finance is needed to establish a business, to run it, to moderate it, to expand it, or diversity it. Etc.

CAPITAL STRUCTURE:

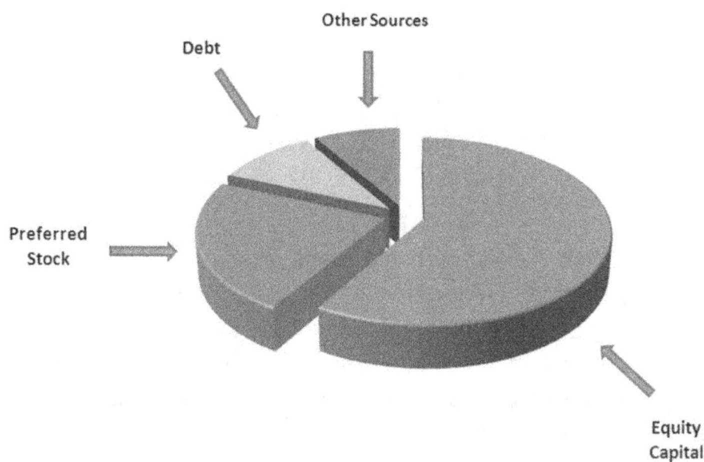

Capital structure refers to the mix between owner funds (equity) and borrowed funds (debt).

Capital structure will be said to be optimal when the proportion of debt and equity is such that it results in an increase in the value of the equity shares.

Debt equity ratio=debt/equity

◆ **Factor affecting capital structure**

1. Cash flow position

2. Cost of that

3. Return on Investment

4. Interest coverage ratio [formula=EBIT/INTREST]

5. Control

6. Tax Rate

7. Flexibility

8. Stock market conditions

9. Regulatory frame work

Financial Leverage:

The inclusion of the fixed cost capital along with equity share capital in the capital structure is called "financial leverage".

It may be favorable or unfavorable

<u>Formula of financial leverage is:-</u> **EBIT / EBT**

TRADING ON EQUITY:

Meaning- Trading on equity means to raise fixed cost capital (borrowed capital and preference share capital) on the basis of equity share capital so as to increase the income of equity shareholders. Although it is possible only when the rate of return of the company is greater than the rate of interest on borrowed capital or the rate of dividend on preference shares.

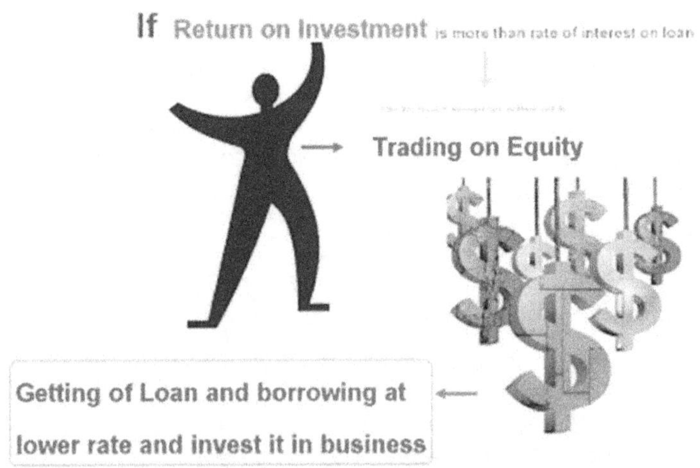

☞ **Trading on Equity**

✂ **FAVOURABLE FINANCIAL LEVERAGE**

	Company 'X'	Company 'y'
Share capital	10,00,000	4,00,000
Loan @ 15% P. a.	-----	6,00,000
Total capital	**10,00,000**	**10,00,000**
Profit before interest and tax (30% ROI)	3,00,000	3,00,000
Less: interest (15% of 600000)	-----	90,000
Profit before tax	3,00,000	2,10,000
Less: tax @ 50%	1,50,000	1,05,000
Profit after tax	1,50,000	1,05,000

$$\text{Rate of return on share capital} = \frac{\text{Profit after tax}}{\text{Share capital}} \times 100$$

$$\text{Company X:} \quad \frac{\text{Rs } 150000}{\text{Rs } 1000000} \times 100 = \textbf{15\%}$$

$$\text{company Y:} \quad \frac{\text{Rs } 105000}{\text{Rs } 400000} \times 100 = \textbf{26.25\%}$$

It is clear from this example that shareholder of the company 'Y' earn higher rate of return than company 'X' due to the debt/ loan component in the total capital and because ROI (30%) is greater than rate of interest (15%)

✂ **UNFAVORABLE FINANCIAL LEVERAGE**

	Company 'X'	Company 'y'
Share capital	10,00,000	4,00,000
Loan @ 20% P. a.	-----	6,00,000
Total capital	**10,00,000**	**10,00,000**
Profit before interest and tax (15% ROI)	1,50,000	1,50,000

Less: interest (20% of 600000)	-----	1,20,000
Profit before tax	1,50,000	30,000
Less: tax @ 50%	75,000	15,000
Profit after tax	**75,000**	**15,000**

$$\text{Rate of return on share capital} = \frac{\text{Profit after tax}}{\text{Share capital}} \times 100$$

$$\text{Company X: } \frac{\text{Rs } 75000}{\text{Rs } 1000000} \times 100 = \textbf{7.5\%}$$

$$\text{company Y: } \frac{\text{Rs } 15000}{\text{Rs } 400000} \times 100 = \textbf{3.75\%}$$

FIXED CAPITAL:

Investment in fixed assets for longer duration is called "fixed capital" It must be financed through long term sources of capital.

Eg: - purchase of goodwill, machinery, Land.

◆ **Factor affecting requirement of fixed capital**

   1. Nature of business (manufacturer, trader, service provider)

2. Scale of operation (big, medium or small)

3. Choice of technique (machine or labour)

4. Technology upgradation

5. Diversification (expansion)

6. Growth prospects

7. Level of collaboration

WORKING CAPITAL:

The amount invested in current assets i.e. cash, bills receivable, debtors, bank etc to facilitate smooth day to day working operation of the business is called "working capital"

These are of two types:-

GROSS WPORKING CAPITAL:

It refers to investment in all the current assets such as cash B/R prepaid expenses inventories etc.

NET WORKING CAPITAL:

It refers to excess of current assets over current liability.

N.W cap=CA-C.L

◆ **Factor affecting requirement of working capital**

1. Nature of business
2. Scale of operations
3. Business cycle
4. Seasonal factors
5. Production cycle
6. Credit allowed
7. Credit availed
8. Availability of raw material

TRADING ON EQUITY:

The use of more debt along with equity share. In the capital structure with a view to increase 'earning per share' is called 'trading on equity'

The equity shares are used as a base to raise loans and debentures; hence the term 'trading on equity' is used.

Eg-firm may choose to have only debt portion in capital or only equity portion or partly debt and equity.

OPERATING CYCLE:

Operating cycle is the period between acquisition of raw materials and the collection of cash from receivable.

Longer the operating cycle, larger will be working capital requirement.

BUSINESS CYCLE:

Business cycles are the conditions of business position or market situation.

e.g. - in case of boom condition, business activities expand, as a result the working capital requirement will be larger. In case of recession period working capital requirement will be less.

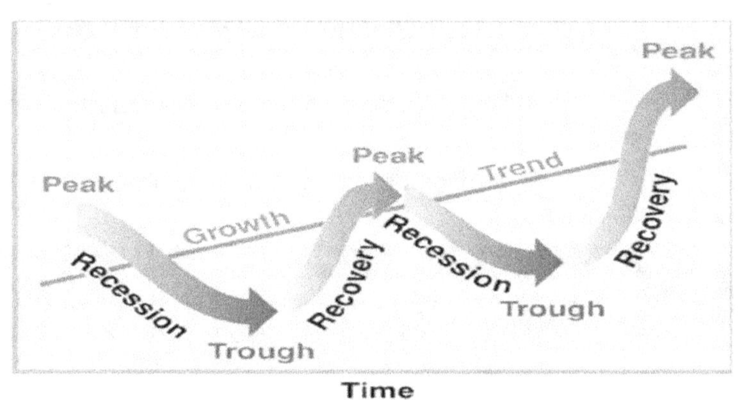

From Author- The greatest mistake –giving up, the greatest blessing- good health, the greatest handicap-egoism, the greatest loss –loss of self confidence...

FINANCIAL MARKET: - (5 to 8 marks)

A financial market is a market for the creation and exchange of financial assets.

It helps in mobilization of saving and channeling them into the most productive uses.

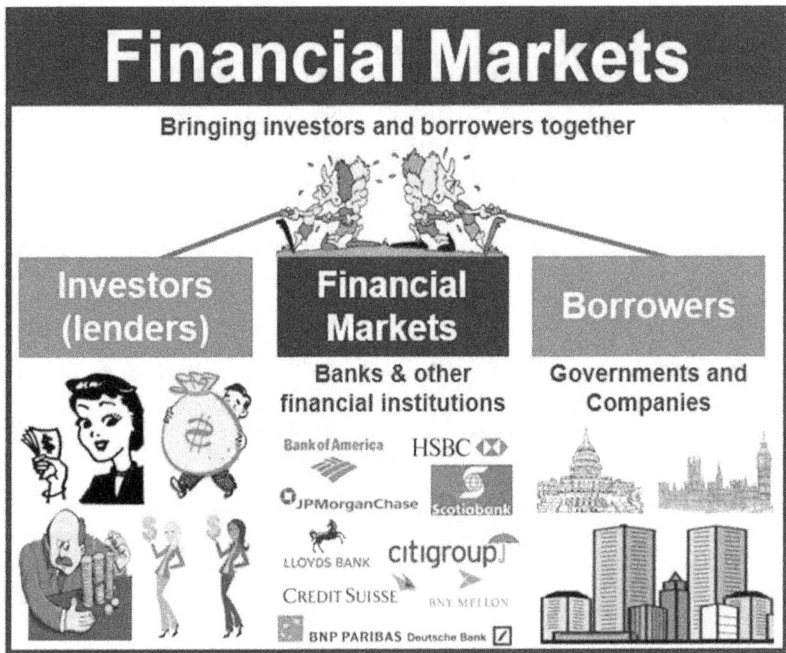

A financial market acts as link between the savers and the investors by mobilizing funds between them.

Eg-banks, insurance company, stock exchange etc

◆ **Functions of financial market**

1. Mobilization of saving and channelizing into the most productive uses

2. Facilitate price discovery

3. Provide liquidity to financial assets

4. Reducing the cost of transaction

�֎ **Types of financial market**

Market	Money market (short term)	Capital market (long term)
Meaning	Money market is a market for short term funds. It deals in monetary assets whose maturity period is up to one year. Eg.treasury bill, call money, commercial paper, commercial bill and COD	Capital market refers to facilities and institutional arrangement through which medium-term and long term funds are raised and invested. The maturity period of these securities is
		more than one year. Eg-debt, equity, mutual fund and loans
Participants	RBI, NBFC'S, commercial banks etc.	Corporate entities, stock exchanges, development banks, commercial banks, foreign investor.
Investment outlay	Require huge sum of money as the instruments are quite expensive. Eg:-treasury bill min for 25000/-	Does not require huge financial outlay as the value of securities is generally low.ie 10 or 100/-
Liquidity	High degree of liquidity due to short term	Less liquid due to long term
Safety	Safer with minimum risk of default ie LOW RISKY	Riskier both respect to return and principal payment ie HIGH RISK
Expected return	Return is less	Higher return for investors

✂ **Money market instrument :-**

Call money (1)	Treasury bill (2)	Commercial bill (3)	Commercial paper (4)	Certificate of deposit (5)
(1) Commercial banks barrow Minimum cash balance CRR	Issued by the RBI on behalf of the central government	A commercial bill is a bill of exchange	Commercial paper is an instrument issued by large and creditworthy companies to raise short –term funds	CD are short –term unsecured negotiable instruments issued by commercial banks or development financial institution to individuals corporations and companies
2) 15 Days	Assured returns negligible risk of default	It is a short –term negotiable and self –liquidating instrument Is called a trade bill	It is an unsecured negotiable promissory note having maturity period of 15 day to one year	
3) Call rate	Amount 25,000 Treasury bills are also known as zero coupon bonds since	Drawer drawee payee	At a discount and redeemed at par	They are issued during period of tight liquidity
(4)	Issue price is less than the redemption value		The purpose of issue of a commercial paper is to provide short –term funds for seasonal and working capital needs e.g., bridge financing	Mobilize a large amount of money for short periods

MONEY MARKET:

Money market is a market for short term funds which deals in monetary assets whose period of maturity is UP to one year. These assets are close substitute for money.

E.g. cheque, demands draft.

CAPITAL MARKET:

It refers to the market where long term funds, both debt and equity are raised and invested.

PRIMARY MARKET:

A primary market is also known as the "new issue market" it deals with new securities being issued for the first time.

SECONDARY MARKET:

The secondary market is the market for the sale and purchase of previously issued securities, i.e. existing securities are traded.

The stock exchange or stock markets represent the secondary market for securities.

✄ **Difference between primary and secondary market:-**

Primary market	Secondary market/ stock exchange
1. It deals with the securities being issued first time	There is trading of existing securities only.
2. Only buying of securities takes place in the primary market. Securities cannot be sold by the investor	Buying and selling of securities takes place on the stock exchange.

3.	Securities are sold directly by the company to investor (or through intermediary)	Ownership exchanged between investors. Company is not involved at all.
4.	Flow of funds is from savers to investor.	Enhances encashability of securities.
5.	Price determine by management of the company	Price depends on demand and supply of the securities.
6.	There is no fixed geographical location	Located at specified places. [BSE ,NSE DSE etc]

◆ **Method of flotation of new issue in the primary market**

1. Offer through prospectus (IPO)

2. Offer for sale (through broker)

3. Private placement (not for all)

4. Right issue (to existing holders)

5. e-IPO (online issue)

STOCK EXCHANGE:

A stock exchange is an institution which provides a platform for buying and selling of securities.

Stock exchange facilitates the exchange of a security (share, debenture, etc) into money and vice versa.

e.g.:-BSE NSE etc.

◆ **Functions of stock exchange**

1. Provide liquidity and marketability of existing securities
2. Determines price of securities
3. Ensure safety of transaction
4. Contribute to economic growth
5. Spread equity cult
6. Provide scope for speculation

◆ **Trading procedure in stock exchange-[how to purchase share] (pizza delivery)**

1. Selection of broker (Sharekhan, religare, zerodha, Kotak etc)
2. Opening demit account
3. Placing the order
4. Executing the order
5. Settlement

◆ **Document Required For Opening DMAT Account**

☞ PAN number (this mandatory)

☞ Residential status (Indian/NRI).

☞ Bank account details.

☞ Depository account details.

☞ Name of any other broker with whom already registered.

◆ **Advantages of electronic trading system or screen-based trading-**

1. ensure transparency

2. increase the efficiency of information

3. increase efficiency of operation

4. improve the liquidity of the stock market

5. provide a single trading platform

◆ **DEMATERIALIZATION**

It is a process where securities held by the investor in the physical form are cancelled and the investor is given an electronic entry or number so that she/he can hold it as an electronic balance in an account.

The process of holding securities in an electronic from is called "dematerialization".

◆ **DEPOSITORY**

Depository is an institution/organisation which hold securities in electronic form, in which trading is done.

It works just like a bank who keep custody of customer money.

In India there are two depository: - **NSDL. CDSL.**

NSDL is the first and largest depository presently operational in India.

NATIONAL STOCK EXCHANGE: (NSE)

National stock exchange is the latest, most modern and technology driven exchange. It was set up in early 1992 by leading financial institutions, banks, insurance companies and other financial intermediaries.

OVER THE COUNTER EXCHANGE OF INDIA: (OTCEI)

OTCEI is a company incorporated in 1990 under the companies' act 1956.

It provides listing facility for small companies with paid up capital of less than 3 Crores.

SEBI (SECURITIES AND EXCHANGE BOARD OF INDIA)

It was set up in 1998 to, regulate the functions of the securities markets, provide adequate protection to investors and thus to create an environment to facilitate mobilization of adequate resource through securities market.

It is a body corporate having a separate legal existence and perpetual succession.

◆ **Objective of SEBI-**

1. To protect the right and interests of investors

2. To prevent trading malpractices like price rigging, insider trading etc

3. To regulate stock exchange and securities exchange

4. To provide a market place in which the issuer can raise finances in an easy manner.

✂ **Functions of SEBI.... (PRD)**

PROTECTIVE FUNCTIONS (for Investor)	REGULATORY FUNTIONS (for Market)	DEVELOPMENT FUNTIONS (for market)
Prohibit fraudulent and unfair trade practices	Registers brokers and sub brokers	Train intermediaries
Control insider trading	Regulate take over bids by companies	Conduct research and publishes information
Promote fair practices	Call for information by undertaking inspection	Undertake measure to develop the capital markets.

MARKETING MANAGEMENT (8 TO 12 MARKS)

Marketing management deals with planning, organizing and controlling the activities related to the marketing of goods and services to satisfy the consumer's want.

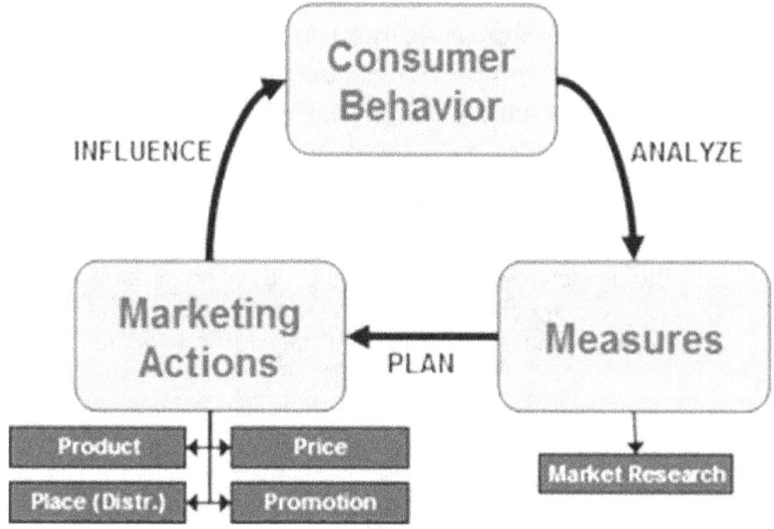

☞   Main focus on 4P's is the essence of marketing management.

☞   What to produce, where to produce, how to produce and in what price it is to be produce.

MARKETER:

If customer is the seeker of satisfaction the marketer is the deliverer or provider of satisfaction.

E.g. HUL- lifebuoy soap, close up tooth paste,, Nestle- dairy milk chocolate, Nescafe -coffee

CONSUMER PRODUCTS:

Consumer products which are purchased by the ultimate consumers or users for satisfying their personal needs and desires are referred to as consumer products

E.g. soap, textiles (garments), toothpaste fans etc

INDUSTRIAL PRODUCTS:

Industrial products are those which are used as input in producing other products

e.g.:-CPU, motherboard, engine, battery.

STANDARDISATION:

Standardisation refers to producing goods of predetermined standards, which help in achieving uniformly and consistency in the output. It reduces the need for inspection, testing and evolution of the products.

e.g.: - ISI AGMARK ISO IDA etc.

GRADING:

Grading is the process of classification product into different groups on the basis of some of its important characteristics such as quality, size etc.

E.g.:-cements in 20/kg 50/kg / 80/kg

◆ **Features of marketing:-**

1. Needs and wants

2. Creating a market offering

3. Customer value

4. Exchange mechanism

◆ **Misconception of marketing :-**

Marketing is same thing as "shopping"

Marketing to mean "merchandising"

Marketing and selling are same

✂ **Difference between marketing and selling:-**

BASIS	SELLING	MARKETING
Meaning	Exchange of goods	Identifying customer need and satisfying them
Scope	Limited	Wide
Focus	Transfer of title	Achieve maximum satisfaction of the customer need
Aim	Profit maximization through sales maximization	Profit maximization through customer satisfaction
Start and end	Start after product is developed	Start much before the product is produced what to produce
Strategies	Promotion and persuation	4p's.... (price promotion product place)

◆ **What is marketed?**

1. Goods
2. Services
3. Events
4. Experiences
5. Persons
6. Places
7. Ideas

◆ **Function of marketing/ marketing activities:-**

1. Gathering market information
2. Marketing planning
3. Product designing

4. Standardisation and grading

5. Packaging and labeling

6. Branding

7. Pricing of product

8. Physical distribution

9. Promotion

10. Customer support services satisfy

◆ **Process of marketing management:-**

1. Choosing a target market

2. Getting, keeping as well as growing the customers

3. Creating, developing and communicating superior values for the customers

4. Building the goodwill / reputation

◆ **Marketing management philosophies/concept/orientation**

1. Production concept (jayda banaye)

2. Product concept (accha banaye)

3. Selling concept (promote Karen)

4. Marketing concept (need puri Karen)

5. Societal concept (eco friendly banayen)

Basis	Pro-duction concept	Product concept	Selling concept	Mar-keting concept	Societal concept
1. Start-ing point	Factory	Factory	Factor	Market	Market society
2. Main focus	Quantity of product	Quality per-formance features of product	Existing product	Customer needs	Customer needs and soci-ety's well being

3. Means	Availabil-ity and afford-ability of product	Product improve-ments	Selling and pro-moting	Integrated marketing	Integrated marketing
4. Ends	Profit through volume of production	Profit product quality	Profit through sales volume	Profit through customer satisfac-tion	Profit through customer satisfac-tion and social welfare

MARKETING MIX:

It refers to the combination of four elements, I.e, products, price, promotion and the place known as the four p's of marketing.

PRICE MIX:

Price is the value which a buyer passes on to the seller in lieu of the product or services provided.

Or

Price mix refers to all those decisions which are concerned with price fixation availability of discount, credit policy and period of credit.

◆ **Pricing strategy**

    1.   Market penetrating (charging low price to capture market.)

    2.   Market skimming (setting high price)

◆ **Factor affecting pricing strategy.**

    1.   Pricing objective

    2.   Product cost

    3.   Competition in the market

    4.   The utility and demand

    5.   Governmental and legal regulation

    6.   Marketing method used

PRODUCT MIX:

When a firm becomes a multi-product company the total no. of product and items it offers to the market is called product mix.

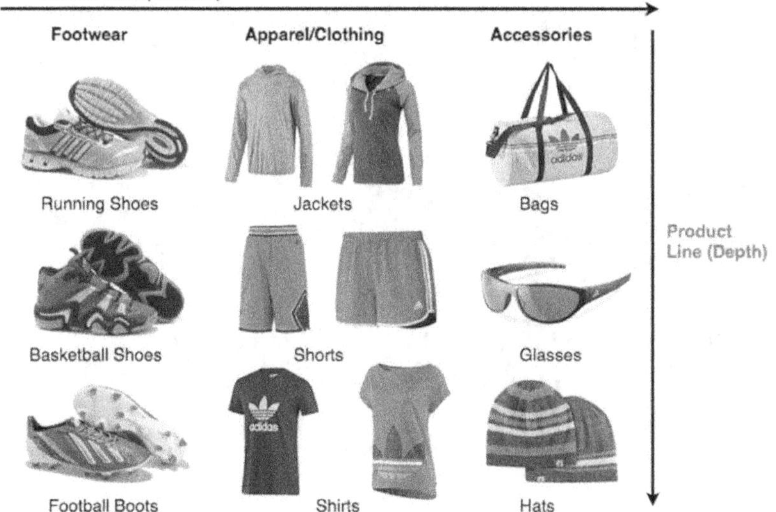

✂ Distinguish Between The 'Products' and 'Production'

Basis of Different	Product	Production
(i) Focus	Focus is on good quality products.	Focus is on production.
(ii) Means	Product improvements	Easy availability of products.
(iii) Ends	Profit through providing better quality products.	Profit through large scale production.

BRANDING:

Branding can be defined as the process of giving a name or a sign or a symbol etc to a product.

e.g.; - Popular brand name in shoes industry is Reebok, in pen industry is Parker, in car industry BMW.etc

BRAND:

It refers to a special word, symbol, letter or mixture of these.

E.g. lux soap - Here soap is a product but name "lux" is the brand.

BRAND NAME:

It refers to that part of brand which can be spoken.

e.g. - Asian paints, uncle chips etc.

BRAND MARK:

It refers to that part of brand which cannot be spoken but can be recognized easily.

E.g. yog shama of LIC, devil of onida, zuzu of Vodafone.

TRADE MARK:

When a brand is registered under the trade mark act 1999, then it becomes the trade mark.

The trade mark of one company can't used by any other company.

E.g.-Mercedes, jaguar, micromax etc.

◆ **Advantage of Branding:-**

To the marketer	To the Customer
Enable making of new product	Help in product identification
Ease in introduction of new product	Status symbol
Differential pricing	Ensure quality
Help in advertising and display programmes	

◆ **Characteristics of a good Brand name-**

1. Short and easy to pronounce (LG, RIN)
2. Name should be suggestive in nature (HAIR AND CARE, UJJALA)
3. Distinctive (AIRCEL, AIRTEL)
4. Staying power (PARLE.G, COCA COLA)
5. Capable of being register
6. Meaning should be clear (NOVA)

PACKAGING:

Packaging refers to the act of designing and producing the container or wrapper of a product.

e.g. - soap comes in paper boxes

Refrigerator or TV comes in hard wood and board cartoons.

◆ **Level/Types of packaging**

1. Primary packaging (toothpaste tube, cream)

2.   Secondary packaging (cream in card board box)

3.   Transportation package (apple in box, pepsi in zaar)

◆ **importance of packaging -benefits / function**

1.   Product identification

2.   Product protection

3.   Product promotion

4.   Product differentiation

5.   Easy handling

6. Rising standard

7. Innovational opportunity

LABELLING:

A label is a tag which is found on the package providing all the information regarding product and its producer.

e.g. - name of medicine, manufacturer name, date of manufacture, expir date etc.

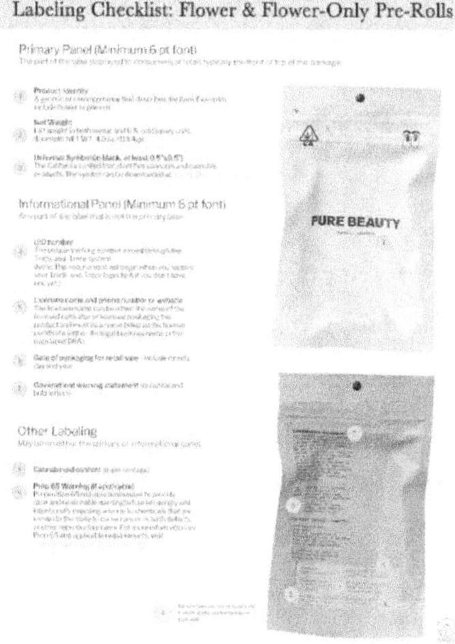

◆ **Functions or importance of labeling**

1. Describe the product and specify its contents(MFR MRP, expiry date)

2. Identification of the product or brand (logo of product)

3. Grading of product (brook bond green and red label)

4. Help in promotion of product (20% extra and cash back tag)

5. Providing information required by law (smoking warning)

Place or physical distribution:

It refers to a set of decision that need to be taken in order to make the product available to the customer/consumer for purchase and consumption.

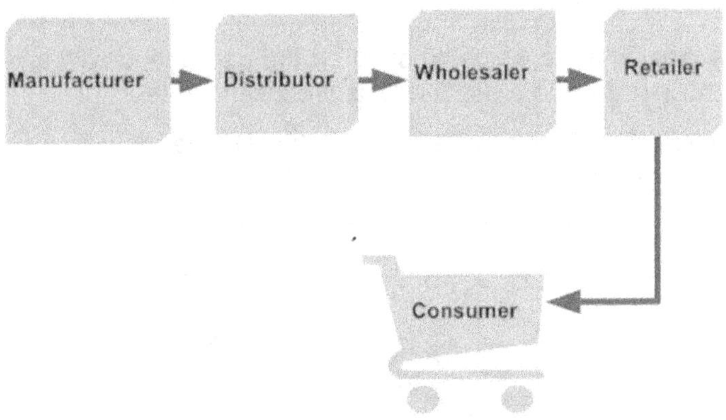

◆ **Level of channel of distribution**

1. Direct channel (zero level) {mac.d sell burger through its own retail shop}

2. One level channel (indirect channel) [maruti sell its car through its approved retail shop]

3. Two level channel (indirect channel) {sell through wholesalers]

4. Three level channel (indirect channel) (agent also included)

◆ **Functions performed by channels of distribution**

1. Sorting

2. Accumulation

3. Allocation

4. Assorting

5. Product promotion

6. Negotiation

7. Risk taking

◆ **Component of physical distribution:-**

1. Order processing
2. Transportation
3. Warehousing
4. Inventory control

✄ **Factor affecting channel of distribution:-**

Market factors	Product related factors	Company character/ related factors	Competitive factors	Environment factors
Size of market	Nature of product	Financial strength of the company	Competitive channel of distribution	Economical and legal constraints
Geographical issues	Perishable or nonperishable	Degree of control		
Size of order	Unite value of product			
	Product complexity			

PROMOTION MIX:

It deals with informing the customer about the firm's product and persuading them to purchase the same.

Elements of promotion mix:-

☞ Advertising

☞ Sales promotion

☞   Public Relation

☞   Personal selling

ADVERTISING:

Advertising is any paid form of non personal presentation and promotion of ideas, goods or services by an identified sponsor.

The most common modes of advertising are 'newspaper', 'magazine', 'television' and 'radio'.

◆   **Functions of advertising:-**

1.   Create demand

2.   Educate consumer and makes shopping easier

3.   Enhance consumer confidence

4.   Create better organisational image

5.   Facilitates introduction of new products

6.   Creates customer loyalty

7.   Provides economies of scale

8.   Improves standard of living

◆   **Merits of advertising:-**

(i)   Mass reach

(ii)   Enhancing customer

(iii) Expressiveness

(iv) Economy

◆ **Limitation of advertising:-**

(i)   Less forceful

(ii)   Lack of feedback

(iii) Inflexibility

(iv) Low effectiveness

◆ **Objection to advertising/ criticisms against advertising:-**

1. Add to cost

2. Undermine social values

3. Encourage sale of inferior products

4. Confuses the buyer rather than help

5. Some advertisements are in bad taste

6. Some advertisements makes false claim

✂ **Different media of advertising**

	Media	Advantage	Drawbacks
1.	Newspaper	✔ They offer mass coverage or reach. ✔ Because of large circulation, the average cost per paper becomes very low.	✔ It has very short life of one day only. ✔ Through newspaper, firms can reach literate customers only.
2.	Magazines	✔ The life of advertisement is longer	✔ Less frequency Less flexibility in message. ✔ Dramatisation is not possible.

		Merits	Demerits
		✔ Audience spends more time in reading advertisements in magazines.	
3.	**Television**	✔ This medium is audio-visual. Great dramatisation is possible ✔ It has high reach or coverage	✔ It involves high cost. ✔ Advertisements are shown for a short span only.
4.	**Radio:**	✔ Messages could reach the remotest areas. ✔ Cost is low. ✔ Suitable for illiterate customers also.	✔ It has only autio effect, so it has less attention. ✔ Noise and disturbance bring interruption in message.
5.	**Outdoor:**	✔ Very attractive when designed with electric display. ✔ High visibility and lower cost.	✔ Limited audience. ✔ Short attention span.
6.	**Internet**	✔ Message dramatisation is possible ✔ Interactive media where two-way conversation is possible.	✔ Relatively new media with a low number of users.

PERSONAL SELLING:

Personal selling means –selling "products personally.

It involves oral presentation of message in the form of conversation with one or more prospective customer for the purpose of making sales.

◆ Characteristics / features of personal selling-

1. Personal form of communication
2. Develop personal relationship with the customer
3. Flexible tool of promotion

◆ Merits of Personal Selling

1. Flexibility
2. Direct feedback
3. Minimum wastage

◆ Role of Personal Selling

a. Importance to Businessmen

(i) Effective promotional tool

(ii) Flexible tool

(iii) Minimizes wastage of efforts

(iv) Consumer attention

(v) Lasting relationship

(vi) Role in introduction stage

b. **Importance to Customers**

    (i)   Helps in improving standards of living

    (ii)   Consumers get latest market information

    (iii)   Helps the customers in identifying their needs and wants

    (iv)   Customers get expert advice

c. **Importance to Society**

    (i)   Converts latent demand into effective demand,

    (ii)   Employment opportunities

    (iii)   Career opportunities

    (iv)   Mobility of sales people

    (v)   Product standardisation

◆ **Qualities of a good sales person:-**

1. Physical qualities

2. Mental quality

3. Technical quality

4. Good communication skills

5. Honesty

6. Courtesy

7. Persistent

8. Capacity to inspire trust

✄ ADVERTISING vs. PERSONAL SELLING:-

BASIS	ADVERTISING	PERSONAL SELLING
Nature of communication	Impersonal	Personal
Reach	Large	Limited number
Cost	Cost per person reached very low	Cost per person is very high

Media used	Television, radio, newspaper and magazines	Salesperson
Feedback	Lack	Direct and immediate
Flexibility	Inflexible	Flexible
Time coverage	Cover market in short time	Takes time to cover the entire market.

SALES PROMOTION:

It refers to short term incentives which are designed to encourage the buyers to make immediate purchase of a product or services. It is for the aim to boost the sales of a firm.

◆ **Merits of Sales Promotion**

1. Attention value
2. Useful in new product launch
3. Supplement to other promotional measures

◆ **Limitations of Sales Promotion**

1. Reflects crisis
2. Spoils product image

◆ **Sales promotion activities-**

1. **Rebate** (special price, excess inventory, limited period offer)

2. **Discount** (price less than list price reduced in %)

3. **Refund** (get back money show wrapper)

4. **Product combination** (sim free with phone)

5. **Quantity gift** (extra quantity)

6. **Sampling** (free sample for use)

7. **Contest** (Bourn vita quiz contest)

8. **Lucky draw** (In purchase of special item)

9. **Instant draw and assigned gift** (gold in purchase of soap)

10. **Financing** (emi, installments)

11. **Usable gift** (get extra benefit)

✂ **Company's product and sales promotion techniques used-**

S. NO.	Product	Sales Promotion Alternative	Name of Method
(i)	Cars	Selling the product at 0% interest recovering price in installments.	Full finance @ 0%
(ii)	Washing powder	Distributing samples.	Samples
(iii)	Readymade Garments	Selling the product at 40% discount.	Discount
(iv)	Noodles	Distributing packets of sauce with the product.	Product Combination

PUBLIC RELATION:

Public relation (PR) involves a variety of programmes to promote and protect a company's image or its products in the eyes of the public.

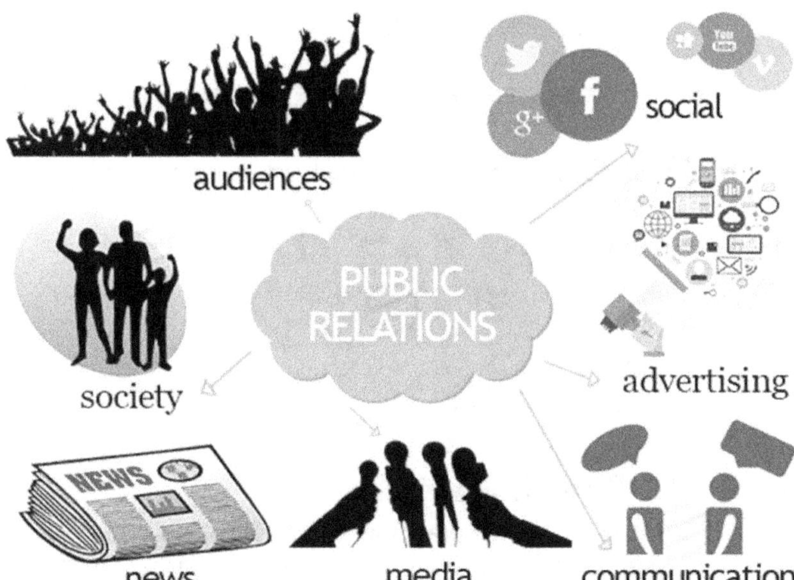

- **Role of public relation / How PR help in achieving marketing objectives:-**

    1. Press relation

    2. Product publicity

    3. Corporate communication

    4. Lobbying (government minister relation)

    5. Counseling (advice top level)

- **Maintaining good public relations also helps in achieving the following marketing objectives:**

    ☞ Building awareness

    ☞ Building credibility

    ☞ Stimulates sales force

    ☞ Lowers promotion costs

Publicity:

Publicity is similar to advertising, in the sense that it is a non-personal form of communication. However,

As against advertising it is a non-paid form of communication.

◆ **Features of Publicity**

1. Publicity is an unpaid form of communication. It does not involve any cost.

2. There is no identified sponsor for the communication as the message goes as a news item.

◆ **Merits of Publicity**

1. Message has more credibility because the information is disseminated by an independent source, e. g. the press in the form of news.

2. Mass reach because message goes in the form of a news rather than direct sales communication.

◆ **Limitation of Publicity**

An important limitation of publicity is that as a medium of promotion, it is not within the control of a marketing firm. The media would cover only those pieces of information which are worthy. Thus, a firm can not use publicity to actively promote its products.

> **From Author-** The main factor which keeps most of us unhappy is that we not only want to be happy, but happier than others.

Consumer Protection Bill 2018

◆ **Who can file a complaint under the consumer protection act 1986:-**

1. Any consumer

2. Registered consumer association

3. CG or SG

4. One or more consumer

5. Legal heir or representative of consumer

◆ **Against whom a complaint can be filed:-**

1. Seller, manufacturer or dealer of goods

2. Provider of services

◆ **Remedies / reliefs available to a consumer:- (*3RC*)**

1. To remove the defect in the goods

2. To replace the defective product

3. To refund the price

4. To pay the compensation

5. Not to offer hazardous goods from sale, etc

◆ **Rights of consumers (case study):-**

Consumer Rights

1. Safety

The right to safe, effective products that have been tested

2. Information

The right to information on how to use the products

3. Choice

The right to have market choices and avoid monopoly

4. Voice

The right to an opinion about how products are made

5. Redress

The right to legal action if harmed by a business

1. Right to safety (right to be protected against goods)

2. Right to be informed (right to have complete information about the product)

3. Right to choose (right to choose from a variety of product at competitive)

4. Right to be heard (right to file a complaint)

5. Right to seek redressal (right to be relief in case of defective goods)

6. Right to consumer education (right to acquire knowledge)

BIS hallmark

Agmark

ISI mark

FPO mark

◆ **Consumer's responsibilities/ duties / obligation to fulfill :-**

1. Buy only standardized product
2. Read labels carefully
3. Know the risk associated with that product
4. Ask for a cash memo
5. File a complaint
6. Be in organize form
7. Aware of the market

✖ **Three tier redressal machinery:-**

	District forums	State commissions	National commission
Set up by	SG	SG	CG
Members	President, two members one of whom must be woman.	President and not less than two members one of whom must be woman	President, four members and one of whom must be woman
Value of goods or services in question	Not exceeds 20 lakhs	1 crore	More than 1 crore
Procedure	Notice to party and sample for testing in lab.	Notice to party and sample for testing in lab.	Notice to party and sample for testing in lab.
Action	Decision on the basis of report	Decision on the basis of report	Decision on the basis of report
Aggrieved party option	Go to state commission within 30 days	Go to national commission within 30 days	Go to supreme court within 30 days

- ◆ **Important Consumer Organisations and NGOs in India**
    1. Voluntary Organisation in Interest of Consumer Education (VOICE), Delhi
    2. Consumer Coordination Council, Delhi
    3. Consumer Protection Council, Ahmedabad
    4. Consumer Guidance Society of India, Mumbai
    5. Consumers' Association, Kolkata

- ◆ **Role of consumer organisations and NGO: - (*life POP*)**
    1. Educating general public
    2. Interest in consumer right
    3. Encouraging customer to protest
    4. Providing legal assistance
    5. Filling complaints in courts
    6. Publishing periodicals
    7. Organizing exhibitions
    8. Producing films in issue

- ◆ **Importance of consumer protection-**

    For organisation –
    a. ... long –term interest of business
    b. ... Government intervention
    c. ... moral justification
    d. ... business uses society's resource

    For consumer –
    a. ... consumer ignorance
    b. ... unorganized consumers
    c. ... widespread exploitation of consumers

- ◆ **Legal Protection to Consumers**
    1. The Sale of Goods Act, 1930
    2. The Essential Commodities Act, 1955

3. The Prevention of Food Adulteration Act, 1954

4. The Standards of Weights and Measures Act, 1976

5. The Trade Marks Act, 1999

6. The Bureau of Indian Standards Act, 1872

7. The Indian Contract Act, 1872

8. The competition Act, 2002

9. The Agricultural Produce (Grading and Marking) Act,1937

◆ Ways and Means of Consumer Protection

1. Government

2. Consumer organisations

3. Consumer awareness

4. Self-regulation by business

5. Business

❑❑❑

From Author- "You can't buy a single moment of life, so live it, cheer it and capitalize each minute of your life"

TIME MANAGEMENT

- Time is the most important resource.
- Time is the capital and not renewal income
- We should remember our true purpose of life to live in this planet.
- Make every day count. Live everyday as if its your last.
- The best to improve yourself is thinking "MY BEST DAYS ARE YET TO COME"

EXAM DAYS TIPS

- Always follow time table and divide each question in minute out of 3 hours.
- Take at least 1 hour sleep before starting new subject exam Preparation.
- Do not use new pen in exam.
- Do not carry question paper at home or tally answers or discuss with friends just forget about it.
- Exercise with your fist for one minute before writing exam.
- Take deep breath in – breath out. And now start writting paper.

TIPS FOR LIFE

- Make a habit of reading newspaper.
- Make habit for early bed and early rise.
- Always respect elders (i.e. family, neighbors' teachers) to get respect in future.
- Be so polite and confident in public place.
- Never keep your problem in mind let it share with your parents, friend, teacher (me) or anybody whom you trust most.
- Think about INDIA, your home Town family and then yourself to make your future happy and bright.
- Before taking any new decision in life think its final impact/result good or bad on your life.

*****GOOD LUCK MY ROCKERS*****

Our past years result that shows our quality of teaching-

BUSINESS STUDIES

2018-2019 - Batch		
S.NO.	NAME	MARKS
1	Sushant	85
2	Gourav	83
3	Muheeb	81
4	Tanmay	75
5	Vishal	72
6	Deepika	72
7	Zameel	72
8	Amit	60
9	Manish	60
10	Roshan	60
11	Stephen	60

Note – This is not the complete list, only exhaustive list.

2017-2018 - Batch		
S.NO.	NAME	MARKS
1	Tanya	94
2	Ashwin	92
3	Nitin	89
4	Monika	88
5	Yogita	82
6	Deepika	81
7	Nitesh	78
8	Aprna	74
9	Ritika	73
10	Anshu	70
11	Abhisek	60

Note– This is not the complete list, only exhaustive list.

2016-2017 - Batch		
S.NO.	**NAME**	**MARKS**
1	Ritika	87
2	Varun Gulati	86
3	Aarti	86
4	Sarul Saji	82
5	Neha	80
6	Pooja	77
7	Poorva	77
8	Sankeri Sarkar	73
9	Rinku	71
10	Sonam	70
11	Shivani Gupta	67
12	Neelam Sharma	62
13	Bhavna Samvedi	60
14	Farheen	60

Note– This is not the complete list, only exhaustive list.

-Thank you so much for choosing me as your teacher.-

By- Dhruvkant Sharma (Tutors and Trainer)

[CA(F), M.Com, PGDM, PGDFT, B.Com (DU)]

-All the best for final examinations-